Sugar Bay

Sugar Bay

Tom Reynolds

Published by Tablo

Table of Contents

Dedication.

*I dedicate this book to my two Grandsons, Eli and Toby
in the hope that anything I may have done right will
encourage them to live good and satisfying lives.*

CHAPTER 1

THE FISHING TRIP

Sandy Horder was the owner and skipper of the *Sugar Bay*. In the time he had been in town, this permanent resident of the prestige suite of the Country Club left an indelible impression of selfless good under the cloak of anonymity. But who was Sandy Horder?

Four patrolling dolphins edged in closer to the big twenty eight foot cruiser as she neared the heads of Port Stephens. Sandy smiled to himself and steered his vessel accordingly to the centre of the gap. There seemed always to be someone watching over him. The big craft tossed and skewed where the ocean waters met the bay, the inboard marine engines growled an expensive muffled anger when the huge brass props spun to their governed limit when contact was broken with the sea. With one hand on the wheel and the other on the power, he skilfully piloted his boat through the tricky entrance of the heads to what had become his paradise.

"Well done Sandy," Maurice Campbell bellowed from below. He was the unchallenged head of the big four. He was always jubilant after a successful mornings fishing in this, The Bay they all called home.

The Skipper eased back on the power and turned toward the unmistakable panorama of Shoal Bay. Once the deck was steady and the engines settled back to their cultured hum

Maurice Campbell stepped out of the lounge area onto the deck. At seventy three, this bow legged ex-farmer from the top of the Hunter Valley was the oldest fisherman on the *Sugar Bay*. Except for his bunged up hips, which made him waddle more than walk, the old farmer was well tanned and in pretty good shape for his age. He grabbed the rail and pulled himself up the five steps to the bridge.

"Hold lunch mother, I'm bringing it home," he said as he slapped the Skipper on the shoulder and looked towards land. "Gee that was a good catch."

"Yes we certainly got amongst them," Sandy replied.

"That dewy you caught wouldn't fit in a milk vat!" the old farmer told Sandy.

"How do you do it?"

"Now, if I told you Maurice…." the sentence always strung out, there was never an answer. Sandy Horder was an unpretentious man who seemed to have it all, but brushed off all the accolades and explanations. "How's Jimmy?" he asked.

"He'll live. I told him if he brings up last night's tea again when I'm catching fish he'll go in after it."

"A bit of seasickness?" the Skipper asked as he looked towards the bay and spun the wheel.

"Bullshit," the old farmer grabbed the bridge railing, "the little bastard was out drinking all night. He did the same thing last week."

Just under ten minutes later Sandy Horder bumped the *Sugar Bay* into the jetty at Shoal Bay. Maurice secured the stern rope and as the reversing props brought the bow in, Sandy grabbed the railing and cleared the five steps onto the deck, expertly flicked the bow rope over the nearest pylon and pulled his beautiful craft gently onto a buffer.

"Righto boys it's safe you can come out now," Maurice Campbell could be a sarcastic old devil, he insisted on doing all the chores around the boat, but left no one in doubt that he had done so.

The 'boys' filed out of the lounge area onto the deck. Walt McEnroe like his millionaire ex farmer mate was also in his early seventies but wasn't as agile. Walt had spent all his life in the Motel business, now called hospitality. He didn't go into business to be hospitable; he had been hiding black money in funny accountants for thirty five years and now was enjoying the fruits of his labour. "Jimmy, land," the over-weight Walt called out.

Next out was Steve Flint he dipped his head slightly as he came through the doorway. He was a six foot two dashing retired Qantas pilot a position he took up after a twenty five year career in the air force. With two retirement packages this quiet calculating man and his wife enjoyed a very comfortable lifestyle in a lovely home unit overlooking the Bay. Steve, who was a keen golfer and fitness fanatic, a routine from his air force days, met the boys most afternoons, but drank only light beer and counted them religiously.

Dick Walker sold his Real Estate business in suburban Newcastle ten years ago when he was sixty and moved into what was then his holiday house with his wife Bev. Like most men who had made their money from nothing and barged through life on sheer determination, Dick Walker had a hard view on everything and always drove the point home. His wise friends stayed away from subjects like politics, religion and social issues and stuck to fishing and sport for the sake of an even conversation. Given the chance Dick would want to change the Australian rugby league coach or bring in a complete unknown for the country's opening bat.

"Don't forget it is Thursday Dick, pension day. Why don't you take Bev to McDonalds?" was how Jimmy Zininski handled Dick Walker. At fifty one this slightly built Australian borne Pole was by far the junior of the group. His parents immigrated to the land of opportunity after the Second World War and like so many of their countrymen headed for the industrial cities like Newcastle with her big steelworks. Like the generations before him, young Jimmy got lost in the crowd for thirty five years until someone offered him a redundancy package. Jimmy's first words to the Personal Manager who went through his submission with him were "Let's go and have a drink."

It took the brash little Pole just three weeks to sell his home in Mayfield, the steel city's heartland, and buy an old run down house with an attached flat just one street back from the water in Shoal Bay. "What about the children," his wife Isa pointed out, "we could help them out?"

"Yeah we could," Jimmy thought for a second, "but I think it is character building if they make their own way in life. Maybe we could let them use the old flat in their holidays."

"You should go home and have a lie down son. You don't look well." Dick treated Jimmy like a mischievous boy.

Sandy Horder was the only one without a past, (or so they thought) saying that he had retired from the iron and steel business in Western Australia after the sudden loss of his wife. A new life and a new start was what he wanted in Shoal Bay, which he christened *Sugar Bay,* hence the name on the boat. The likeable new man in town was accepted and respected without question.

But, who was he?

CHAPTER 2

LIFE ON BULWER STREET

Emit Horsley was born in Perth fifty eight years ago. He was born into a working class society in inner suburbia where all the terraces look the same. In fact as he grew older and started to roam he found that the houses in most of the streets around them had also worked from the same blueprint. They were a society that accepted their lot in life. Employment was usually found in inner city industries or on the wharves, the latter being a bit of a closed shop which forced young Emit into an apprenticeship in the local foundry.

In years to come, the Horsley family and others in their street and suburb who lived in houses without front lawns, council parks or gardens, would be squeezed out. Inner city foundries and mills would be flattened to make way for unit developments and shopping centres. Heritage councils would only step in and save the streets of terraces.

As time moved on rich professionals would move back into the inner city as they had in all the other big capitals of the world.

He looked out to the blue waters of Shoal Bay and remembered the ocean on the other side of the country where he had come from and the very few times that he had played in it as a kid. No. Tranquil, beautiful, natural, places like the seaside were for the privileged with their holiday houses sitting on the sand, with their big cars and their power jobs. They didn't live in Bulwer Street or even in the suburbs. The bosses who owned the businesses that employed the locals came from afar, wherever that was. They were the ones who came in their big cars and left work early. They never got their hands dirty with the labours of industry as they sat in their offices overlooking the work floor. No, very few people in Bulwer Street ever made it out.

Emit looked down, he was thoughtful. It all seemed so long ago. He did the rough calculation again, today was Tuesday. He had checked that on the newspaper before leaving the Motel this morning. That made it four days since he had left Perth.

Nobody would really care, except maybe his two brothers, but because they didn't see that much of each other it could be weeks even months before they found out he was gone. And his wife certainly wouldn't say anything. He could imagine her shrugging her shoulders to inquiring neighbours after a couple of weeks. And his daughter, well he could never do anything right in her eyes.

Emit sat on the park bench looked again to the blue water gently lapping the white sand just a stone throw in front of him. The decision that he had battled with for a couple of years was made for him. Today he became Sandy Horder.

★ ★ ★ ★ ★ ★

The noise and the heat of A.J. Cameron Foundry and Sheet Metal could be felt as soon as you walked in the gate. The big open doors and the four equally large ventilation openings along the top of the building helped the industrial monster breathe out its hot breath and fumes from the open hearth ovens and furnaces. The continual banging of metal on metal to forge a shape, the whirring of the over-head crane, chains being dragged over concrete and the general shouting to be heard over all of this were all in the symphony of sound that Emit accepted for most of his working life.

As a young man he had followed his father into the foundry when he left school as an apprentice fitter and turner. Old foundries like A.J. Cameron that were started in the last century when there was a great need for metal castings, diversified into sheet metal and engineering as a subsidiary when the call for intricate castings started to fall away. The young man's parents were so proud of him when he was accepted as the new apprentice. His position as a tradesman would eventually put him level with his father's position as Foreman Castings Maker.

There were two distinct divisions in A.J. Camerons. The foundry was made up of mainly middle aged men; the young fellows weren't drawn to working long shifts around the furnaces. The other section was the tech men in the sheet metal and engineering division, so called because this small band had to go to Technical College to learn their trade. Emit was a tech man. He enjoyed his work and liked machinery.

When he was eighteen and a third year apprentice, he bought a 1952 Holden, and with management's authorization worked on it at the foundry after hours and on Saturdays. The car had become a bit of a project, with Emit's boss helping out with technical advice and the odd bolt or molding, compliments of the firm. His father was commissioned as

Foreman Castings Maker to mold a special inlet manifold to take the three Stromberg carburettors the young man had saved for months to buy.

He used the lathes and welders in his own time to modify the cylinder head and make a complex extractor system. The high intensity cutting torch allowed the young man to split the original rims on the car and widen them with an extra metal strip. He shortened the springs the same way and with the help of his boss devised a hardened rod linkage to counter the instability force in the rear suspension. Yes, those early years at A.J. Camerons were good times; the young Emit Horsley was a popular young man with a bright future.

The car and Emit were very recognizable around his working class suburb; he had made a statement and attracted other young fellows with a similar passion. He had become the man to talk to if you were going to do something with your car.

He toyed with the idea of leaving A.J. Camerons and to start his own engineering shop specializing in car modifications. But, around that time young Emit started taking out Beatrice Jordon, a girl who also lived in Bulwer Street. She was attracted to his car more as a means of getting out of the street and taking in the movies and cafes in the city. The plan for his enterprise was thus put on hold.

Young Emit Horsley and Beatrice Jordon were married on Beatrice's twenty first birthday. Her mother made the dress and the cake it was truly their day. The small suburban Church and Hall were packed with Jordons and Mulhollands, the latter being the mother's side of the family. After the wedding and the congratulations and a whole lot of back slapping were over, the young couple went to live with Beatrice's parents, just to give them a good start in life.

It took Emit eleven years to save enough money for a deposit on a home of his own. Beatrice insisted it be the one just three doors down from her mother who needed help with her chores now that she was getting older.

The marriage bore only one child, Dorothy, a daughter the spitting image of her mother.

'Life was truly short,' Emit, sitting on the bay side bench thought.

His daughter was in high school by the time he got his own home, which didn't make much difference to their family as mother and daughter spent most of their time from then on with Grandma as she was not only ailing, she was also widowed.

The next six or seven years Emit spent more and more time with his own parents at the other end of Bulwer Street. As maturity crept up on him he saw the quality in his parent's relationship improve and his dwindling.

He lost both of his parents the year Dorothy finished school. Four years later, that was the year his daughter turned twenty one and her Grandmother clocked up eighty, the foundry closed and Emit was paid out a redundancy payment.

Now at forty six and with a metals trade behind him prospects didn't look all that good for the unemployed Emit. Foundries had become ancient history, while metal shops were pushed out to the industrial estates away from the changing landscape of Bulwer Street.

Beatrice Horsley thought the redundancy package was manna from heaven and even thought a trip to Europe for her and Dorothy would be fitting for all the work they had put in nursing Grandma.

Emit took the cheque down to the bank, paid out the mortgage on the house, and put eight thousand dollars into the superannuation fund. The remaining one thousand dollars he gave to his wife with the meaningless words of, "Go and have a good time."

As no metal trades shop was interested in taking on a forty six year old fitter Emit took a job as a cleaner at the local Technical College where he got his trades certificate years earlier. He quite enjoyed the contrast of the work place and the easy routine chores that made up his working day.

Ten years passed and he could see a fairly comfortable retirement light at the end of the tunnel. His first redundancy payout finished the mortgage and enhanced his superannuation package. The third share from his parent's estate topped that package beyond where it normally would be, and for the last ten years he had money taken from his pay as a compulsory saving to put into the Work Credit Union.

Emit didn't expect the money from Beatrice's mother's estate to end up in the superannuation fund. No, she and Dorothy, who was now thirty one and still unmarried, continually talked about the day they would go to Europe. 'That wouldn't be one day too soon,' was one of the bright thoughts in Emit's day. The old girl had just clocked up ninety, and anyone would hold a bet on her reaching the ton.

CHAPTER 3

THE WINDFALL

An unexpected event happened in Emit's life. The change was so dramatic he couldn't believe that this could be happening to him. It was wrong, but it was right for him right now. He grabbed this opportunity with both hands and didn't care about the future.

It all started when Emit decided to buy another car. His wife and daughter deemed this a great waste as he walked to work and the only social activity he had was the Bowling Club on Saturday afternoons, and he always walked there.

Now these two were the authority on waste. There was a continual flow of delivery vehicles to their house bringing the latest time saving devices advertised on the television the previous week. And, no weekend was complete without a Saturday shopping trip into Perth.

Emit had the dream of buying a car, something a couple of years old and tinkering with it as he had years ago with his first Holden. He tried to pick up the pieces of an enjoyable past, a hobby, a purpose, a lost life.

At first he tried to soft soap his wife and daughter with stories like a motoring holiday at Christmas but his was met with, 'and leave poor mum at home by herself? I don't think so.' And, 'we could take your mother for a Sunday drive' was only exposing the dear old lady to those other maniacs on the road. 'She could be killed or even worse!' whatever that could be.

The best course of action he thought was, just go and buy the car. Nobody knew how much he had saved in the credit union in ten years, so if he found the car that fitted his dream he would just buy it.

His criteria were straightforward, it had to be a Holden and it had to be a V8.

After weeks of searching and comparing the 'for sale columns' in the local paper, Emit narrowed the field down to a couple of Holden Statesman. This prestige brand dropped in price significantly after a few years and so offered good value, the extra inclusions being a bonus.

The first such car Emit inspected was beyond his expectations because it was four thousand dollars cheaper than the next one on his list. He thought he would use this as a gauge to measure the others by.

Being only four stops from his own station and a couple of blocks walk at the other end, Emit faked a doctor's appointment and took an afternoon off work. He found the car in a single garage attached to a bungalow type home in a tree lined street quite a bit more upmarket than Bulwer Street.

Emit excitedly rang the doorbell of the quaint cottage. Mrs. Johnson was a tidy looking woman in her early 50's only too keen for the business at hand to be over and done with. When she opened the side door of the garage Emit tried not to gasp at the shiny Burgundy coloured car. 'If the others are better than this one,' Emit thought as he opened the driver's door and smelled the leather upholstery, 'they must be good.'

After a short drive around the surrounding streets, Mrs. Johnson took Emit into the house and over a cup of tea told him it was her late husband's car and she would be pleased if he would take the car and all of its memories. He gave her one hundred dollars that he had withdrawn from the credit union that morning as a holding deposit and promised to return on Saturday with a bank cheque for the balance.

The first thing on Saturday morning, Emit, with the enthusiasm of a young boy bought the new car home. His wife and daughter could see no joy here, only a large petrol guzzler that would be hard to keep clean. Emit brushed aside the guilt he was starting to experience and took the car for another run by himself.

This unselfish man relished in the pleasure his new possession brought him. On the city link freeway he put his foot down and smiled at the feeling of power and the muffled growl as the big V8 surged forward. He touched the buttons on the console that made the windows go up and down. He tried the radio for the first time and was amazed at the different tones that came from speakers which seemed to be everywhere. Even though it was not a hot day he had the air conditioner on at full blast. He couldn't wait to get it back home and really go over it.

Half an hour later, the man who was like a kid on Christmas morning, drove his new car down the back lane and into the yard at the rear of his house, parked it on the concrete apron in front of a small garage and washed it. After that he got the latest television advertised 'time saving device' the wonder vacuum cleaner and started to spruce up the inside of his new pride and joy.

He was rubbing the cleaner head under the front passenger seat when he heard something shoot up the metal pipe. He instinctively switched off the machine retrieved the dust bag and carefully emptied it into the garbage until he found a chrome topped 20 mm nut. The practical ex fitter machinist knew General Motors Holden wouldn't have a chrome plated dome nut under a seat. It must be able to be seen.

He went around the back of the seats and headrests, the rear of the console cowling and all around the door openings and scuff plates. There were no external fixings. He sat on the back seat to contemplate, and found it wasn't secure, in fact it was spongy. He ran his fingers along the edge under the cushion and found what he knew to be a 20mm hole.

Emit smiled and leaned across the seat. On the other side he felt a 20mm dome topped nut. When he got out of the car he noticed that the rear seat sprung up quite a bit on that side and he could see the hole where the missing nut and bolt should be. The whole thing was way out of level as if something was forcing it up. The tradesman in Emit came out, he needed his spanners.

Emit undid the remaining nut, and then applied downward pressure on the seat cushion so he could push the bolt through. He would soon find out what this back seat was hiding. As soon as he took the pressure off the seat cushion, it sprung up level. The rather large rear area of the car allowed Emit to slide in and with his right hand on the floor he lifted the seat from its mount. He choked and fought for breath like a drowning man, but didn't let go of the seat. His eyes were fixed on the prize. If it was an illusion, he was holding onto it by his sheer fixed look.

It must have been at least a minute before he very gently lowered the seat back down. Normally in that position anybody would have experienced shoulder or back ache. Emit felt nothing. Disbelief countered all physical and mental ailings.

He backed out of the car straightened up and nervously looked around for any witnesses. He looked back at the rear seat that now looked like any other, then closed the door and locked the car. He walked down to the house and made a cup of tea, he thanked God that the others were out.

It was two cups of tea and a half an hour later before Emit got his heart rate down and was able to go back to the car again. He unlocked it with the remote and opened the back door. He had a quick look around, then went up and closed the back gate.

This time he was ready, he could assess the situation. He moved both of the front seats forward, then got into the back in a kneeling position. He lifted the back cushion off completely and pushed it out through the open door. The jumbled, cluttered mass of green kicked Emit's heart rate up again. He shook his head in disbelief. The top layers although still in their bundles were scattered over the top of neatly packed rows. Green, a sea of green – one hundred dollar - notes!

Emit picked up a couple of bundles scattered on the top and looked at the rows and rows of neatly packed money. He was looking at tens of thousands, hundreds of thousands, millions!

He quickly counted the notes in one of the bundles in his hand, and then pulled all the loose bundles to one side so that he could count the rows underneath. He was calmer now and counted them off in hundred thousand dollar lots. There were eighteen! He was a Millionaire. He could do whatever he liked. Go wherever he wanted.

He loved the feel of it. He knew he would never give them up. He rationalized his thinking by saying it was his car, therefore it was his money. He started to stack the hoard into cardboard boxes that he had accumulated in the shed, but half way through this exercise and under all the money Emit found two keys, one with the tag, 'Midway Storage Centre' the other a strange brass one.

Emit finished his packing and hid all the boxes in the ceiling of his shed, then went back to the house and looked up the name on the key in the telephone book.

The girl on the phone told Emit that they would be open until 4.30 pm. He in return told her the previous owner of the car's name, and that he had to pick some items up for him from storage.

It was a twenty minute drive across three suburbs and Emit never felt better. He was a new man enjoying his new role. He felt the constraints of habitualness had been severed and he revelled in the thought of his new freedom.

The young girl in the office of Midway Storage Centre remembered the phone call and directed Emit to shed 39.

Even though there was no one around Emit parked the big car across the front of the roller door. Whatever was in there would be treated as top secret. He slowly turned the key and controlled the raising of the door; there in front of him was a mess. His first instinct told him that this was common household junk in storage, but he moved through it anyway.

There was tired garden furniture and old tools, a low boy that proved to be empty, chairs that looked unsafe, things were just thrown in. Emit pushed half empty boxes of clothes and books aside as he made his way over to the camphor chest on the side wall near the back of the shed. Next to that there was a neat stack of storage covered with a tarpaulin. The chest was secured with a decent pad lock keeping safe its treasure. He took the keys from his pocket and looked at the brass key on it. The puzzle was too easy. The key went straight in and turned.

Emit almost went into cardiac arrest again as the old camphor chest gave up her secrets.

The large painting which couldn't lay flat looked original. There was something familiar about the stick drawings. He picked up two smaller colourful outback landscapes, the name in the corner guaranteed value. Lying flat on the bottom of the chest was an unusual seascape. It took a while to find the artist's signature.

'This bloke was into big stuff' Emit thought, backing away from his latest find. He looked at the boxes on the wall and pulled the tarpaulin down as a magician would. The top two fell spilling their contents of beautiful green bundles over the concrete floor.

Emit left the storage with eight boxes of one hundred dollar notes, two Norman Lindsay stick drawings, two Pro Harts and a Dobell seascape. 'They can have the rest,' the new opportunist thought, with all this money and a few irreplaceable Australian paintings he can really go to bigger things.

That night after tea, Emit went back up to his shed. The two women thought he was just playing with his car, instead he was arranging his big move. The travel section of The West Australian lay open on the bonnet of the Statesman depicting the Shoal Bay Country Club. "When you're on the east coast…."

Emit feeling so exhilarated by his find, counted and stacked the money into twelve boxes. Most fitted nicely into the large boot area of the car. The remaining four he sat on the floor in the back.

In all there was ten million dollars, all in one hundred dollar notes.

The five paintings he wrapped in old blankets individually and packed carefully into a suitcase. This, he sat on top of the boxes and allowed himself a quick smile at the answer to the question. "What have you got in the suitcase?"

"Oh, just a couple of Norman Lindsay's, a Pro Hart and a Dobell!"

That left the whole rear area of the car for his personal affects, he could think of nothing he wanted to take from Bulwer Street.

The next morning being Sunday, Emit Horsley had a casual breakfast by himself and read the paper. After his wife had left to go to Grandma's house he hurriedly went to his room, grabbed the overnight bag he had packed the night before with a couple of changes of clothes and went to the back shed. All the while he kept a vigilant eye peeled as this uncharacteristic act would be unexplainable. He backed the car out, closed the shed door and the back gate. He didn't even take a last look at the family home he would never see again.

CHAPTER 4

THE SCAM

John Thomas Johnson worked in the State Department of Treasury in the financial district of Perth. Although Manager of Daily Clearance sounded a high powered position, John Thomas 'Johnno' Johnson regarded himself as a glorified Bank teller with a Masters' Degree in Economics. It was a pretty average job.

He, like all the other 'suits' in his building, carried the daily paper and a cut lunch in his very impressive attaché case which was all part of 'the uniform'. The position entailed exactly what the name implied. It was a Clearance Centre for all computer driven and written transactions. This meant every monetary deal that came through the state of Western Australia was handled by this Clearance Centre. They matched funds and promissory notes with the appropriate currencies.

Because there were always fluctuations in international currencies and clearance took around three days, the value of whatever currency the department was dealing in would be locked in immediately, leaving no room for deviation.

The two basement levels of the State Office Tower were for currency recycling. All notes have a limited life and so are constantly sorted at all Bank branches and sent to this facility for replacement. This was called Bank Note Rejuvenation.

Johnno Johnson watched the currency moves on his monitor every day of his working life and put himself in an imaginative trading situation when big deals came up.

When the brave entrepreneurs of the West were taking over the great Australian corporations splitting them and selling the subsidiaries, Johnno would put on his imaginary trading hat and work out the deal with another currency, mostly the British pound. He was always right, and the difference on the deal over three days could be up to several hundred thousand dollars.

It was a game. You couldn't do it, because you couldn't get the money out. Not that he wanted to, Johnno was an honest man.

As time went on and computers took over more of the work, departments amalgamated. Johnno now found himself in a duel role, in charge of the Clearance House, and Bank Note Rejuvenation.

In this new roll the now dual manager oversaw old banknotes brought into the building via an armed vehicle, transferred into a lift and taken to the basement. Everything was sorted checked and signed off on. They were bought off each individual Bank. Then new notes were resold to the same Banks.

Every afternoon at four o'clock he would go down to the basement and check the amount of money on the monitor that had come in for transfer, enter his password and transfer the amount to a holding account, then direct deposit the amount to each Bank involved.

New notes came in every day and were shipped out to the Banks in the reverse order with the Banks then buying the new notes from the department in the same way.

There were truck-loads of money going up and down this lift all day.

Even though Bank Note Rejuvenation handled hundreds of millions of dollars in notes, the sorting, counting and bundling was all automated. The physical handling of money was done in lots, half lots and quarter lots. The men who handled the product, carried, counted and stacked sealed boxes, a bit like stacking bricks only lighter.

About two months into his dual management position, Johnno, after countless dummy runs, took his chance and tested his wit against the world. He switched currencies out of the Russian Ruble into the British Pound on a huge minerals deal. It wasn't as if it was a wild shot in the dark. It could be likened to Tiger Woods chipping out of the sand trap straight into the hole. Not a fluke, a practiced shot.

He pushed the lever and put his plan into reality.

The lever was the button on his keyboard. This transferred the transaction from the Ruble to the Pound. In the three days it took to clear, the Pound strengthened giving the manipulator more than he had estimated; and then the man simply transferred the surplus funds to gold, being the international currency which could then be held against the account of the Bank Note Rejuvenation. Now he had a small Bank operating inside the Bank.

The challenge now was to get the funds out of the basement before they were checked off for disposal. This didn't pose a problem either. He just got into the habit of carrying an old money carton with him on his daily excursion to the basement. This was always filled with papers and documents relating to his work, well that is what is assumed.

On his first movement of funds from the basement to his upstairs office, Johnno deliberately dropped the carton in front of the guard on the door and feigned embarrassment as he got down to pick up the loose papers. Each time he came past the guard after that on the way out, the old carton was filled with notes, hundred dollar notes.

For two months the Pound rallied along with the US dollar and the Ruble fell. Sometimes just for the heck of it, this high roller of fraudsters would switch to US dollars, though not always as profitable it added spice to the game. On his good days Johnno with all of this money could be heard singing God Save the Queen while walking up from the basement with the familiar carton under his arm.

All good things, as we know come to an end. And all good fraudsters get found out. It's never their timing, but if you look back, there is an event that changes what we had taken for the norm. In Johnno Johnson's case one day there was a small skirmish on a Russian border somewhere, and the Ruble and the British Pound swapped places. Unfortunately for Johnno this event started the day he did a currency switch on a big oil deal.

On day two he was out of pocket $1,200,000-00. He panicked. Money wasn't his problem, why just last week he went out and bought five very expensive Australian paintings and he had millions stacked away in that storage shed.

The problem was getting the money, all those notes, back into the building, and not only that, he needed urgently to square the books. But squaring the books! How do you explain $1,200,000-00 in unaccounted for notes? If that is what it ends up on, on day three.

Fear struck this usually unfazed man on the night of the second day. He had stacked $1,800,000-00 from his storage shed under the back seat of his Holden Statesman car. As he was loading the cash in he realized that the only thing that could save him was a reversal of the currencies. He hurriedly screwed the back seat down locked the shed and started to drive home.

It was nine o'clock when Johnno stopped at a garage to pick up a soft drink. He couldn't understand the dryness in his throat and the continual wiping of the sweat beads from his forehead. He shook slightly as he handed over his cash at the counter and felt that all the eyes in the place were on him.

He had just turned out onto the road again when he spotted a patrolling police car. The now contrite fraudster frantically grabbed for the forgotten seatbelt and spilled his drink.

Terror overtook fear in those few seconds and Johnno Johnson's body could not handle the huge emotional stress put on it. His last act was to steer his car to the safety of a drive way.

About that same time in the northern hemisphere day traders were taking positions on the revitalized Russian Ruble. It seemed the initial drop was a splash in the pan, and everyone expected values to be back to normal by the end of trading.

In the days that followed Johnno Johnson's death, Carl Betz, Manager Domestic Business, assumed the temporary dual role of Manager of Daily Clearance and Bank Note Rejuvenation at the State Department of Treasury in Perth's financial district.

His first problem was a $50,000-00 excess on a three day clearance for the Russian oil deal that Johnno was looking after. It wasn't that there were any funds missing, the account was over by $50,000-00 and in bank business this is just as bad.

Had Johnno still been alive he would have creamed off $50,000-00 a small amount by his previous works, transferred it to Bank Note Rejuvenation as he had done in the past and carried the money out in his old carton.

Carl Betz was puzzled, there must be an explanation. He typed the figures into his computer again. Again the balance was out exactly $50,000-00 which was only a small percentage in the $50 million deal.

He smiled to himself. If this was a grand fraud scheme it wasn't working, they're putting the money in. He went back to the beginning of the transaction and saw the switch from the Ruble to the Pound. Carl Betz then bought the conversation table up on his screen and punched in the numbers. It was $420,000-00 in the black. He then went back to the end of the deal.

After the big plunge on days one and two the Pound did a reversal and went straight up past the break even line to be exactly $50,000-00 in the black by close of trade on day three.

Carl Betz had found a crook, and he was to go to his funeral tomorrow morning.

It took three months for the auditors to issue a report showing that the department was $50,000-00 over in its transactions for the year. This was due to inappropriate currency dealings by an employee.

Carl Betz knew, and the auditors knew, by checking back on Johnno Johnson's work over the period of currency switches, that in fact $10,400,000-00 was creamed off in inappropriate currency dealings. The money was never found. Nobody was out of pocket.

CHAPTER 5

A NEW IDENTITY

Emit Horsley blew into Port Stephens just on a year ago
after he had driven for four days from the other side of the
country. Just himself, his recently acquired car, and a head full
of thoughts. He had spent the previous night and most of the
afternoon in Newcastle where his great transformation had
taken place.

He had booked into a cheap Motel with only an old
overnight bag which contained the last of his change of
clothes. He paid for the room with a hundred dollar note and
got directions to the places he needed to go. His first stop was
the suburban hairdresser, his unkempt seventies style hair was
to be attended to.

"How do you like that?" the barber asked as he stood back
and admired his work, then casting his eyes to the mass of hair
lying on the floor.

"No, take it off the ears and shorter on the top, then knock
the beard off."

It was another half an hour before the complete change
was accomplished.

"You're a different man," the barber remarked as he took a
hundred dollar note from his customer. "I'd put a bit of cream
on that face of yours it's a long time since it has seen the sun,"
he advised.

As Emit walked back towards his car he stopped several times to look in the shop windows. He wasn't looking for anything, just admiring his own reflection. 'The old Emit Horsley was fading away.' he thought.

The shop assistant at David Jones didn't realize he was on a winner when the customer in the jeans and tee shirt headed for the designer rack. The stranger chose wisely in fit and coordination. The clothes he chose were smart and casual, light trousers in beige or white, coloured polos, conservative stripes and checks in long sleeve shirts. The type of wardrobe you would wear in a resort. They were all paid for in cash, in one hundred dollar notes.

That first glimpse of Port Stephens coming in over the hill knocked Emit's heart rate up a couple of beats. He smiled like an excited child at the sight of the water between and over the tops of buildings. It was mid-week and the morning traffic was light. He parked his car in the main street and walked down the hill towards the water.

The main street intersected with another road which followed the water in both directions. "Which way is it to Shoal Bay Sir?" Emit asked a passer-by in a new cultured tone that befitted his new clothes.

"Just follow the water around, you'll know it when you get there."

There was urgency in Emit's step as he headed back up the hill to his car. He had come right across the country for this, his dream was about to be realized.

A few kilometres drive to his destination took Emit Horsley fifteen or twenty minutes. He stopped several times to look at the water and the views on one side, then across the road to the houses that overlooked it. "What a beautiful place," he said aloud each time he stopped.

Emit knew he was almost at his objective when he got a full view of the Heads. As he drove he scanned the gallery where people lived in home units, cottages, and caravans just to gaze at their picture of heaven. He saw the jetty stretch from the footpath over the white sand to the deep water with its game fish gantry standing like a statue on the end.

Out beyond this in deeper water were the yachts, the big white cruisers, crafts of all kinds waiting at their moorings. A couple of small outboards were already making waves, one with water skiers in tow, another heading for the gap, rods racked vertically for a day's fishing in the outside waters.

Emit grabbed the first parking space he saw and walked along the park grass towards the jetty, not taking his eyes off the majestic building across the road. This is what he most wanted to see. The buildings took up about a third of the block on mass, along the waterfront; he pulled a wallet from his back pocket and unfolded a picture cut from the travel section of The West Australian. 'When you're on the east coast treat yourself to a bit of luxury at the Country Club Shoal Bay,' the caption read.

He looked at the black and white picture, then at the building. It was as if it had just been taken. The cane lounge had couples sitting behind huge floor to ceiling windows having a late breakfast, others indulged in the morning paper, or in conversation. All took the time to occasionally glance out at the beautiful slow moving waters of Shoal Bay.

He walked past the beer garden and the corner bar, they were like the Sydney cricket ground on a Sunday morning with the cleaners moving around quietly about their jobs. These places needed only the crowd and the characters for atmosphere.

Emit folded the small piece of paper and walked over to a park bench facing the water; it was a sad moment, a big decision, a new life.

CHAPTER 6

THE COUNTRY CLUB

Emit Horsley sat back on the bayside seat and pondered his future once again. In the four days since he had found the money, there had been no reports of anyone missing it, and since it seems to have had no legitimate past it would be hard to pass off in some investment. Emit smiled to himself, what a nice predicament. He had a simple plan, but first he had to book into The Shoal Bay Country Club and create a new identity for himself.

"Can I help you?" The attractive receptionist asked the distinctive looking newcomer standing before her, as he took in the unfamiliar pleasant surroundings of the hotel foyer. The girls on reception duty got to know straight away the long stayers with money. They were usually handsome, wore expensive casual clothes, carried little luggage, and if there was a woman with them, she looked as if she had just stepped off the cover of Vogue.

"Yes," Emit said slowly and definitely, "nice place you have here."

"We love it," the young lady wisely let the stranger sell the product to himself. The long stayers were cream for the hospitality industry, they paid the same as anyone else, and because the room didn't have to be booked again they were less trouble.

"Yes," Emit repeated stroking his chin as he cultivated his new character. "I'd like to book in if I may?"

"Will you be staying long sir?"

"Oh a couple of months I should expect."

'We have got a beauty here,' the young receptionist thought, this is the next resident for the upstairs suite. "We have a lovely suite on the northern corner," she gestured up to her left, "Would you like me to show it to you Sir?"

"It sounds nice I'll take it."

"Certainly Mr......?"

"Horder," Emit came up with the name as he was driving along the waterfront earlier on, he had seen it on the side of a removalist truck.

"Sandy Horder" and the Christian name suited his new persona, that of the indifferent retiree.

"Yes Mr. Horder." The girl felt as though she was in the presence of an important person. The name had that sort of ring to it. She started to fill out a registration card, and then looked up at the new guest.

"What dates should I put in Mr. Horder?"

"Make it two months from today."

"Do you have any I.D?" the girl went about her job.

"Must we?" Emit hadn't thought of this. He pulled a roll of one hundred dollar notes from his trousers pocket in his new casual air.

"I'd like to pay a month in advance. If you could let me know when that's nearly up I'll sign a new contract."

"Certainly Mr. Horder."

The receptionist asked the usual questions as her fingers expertly typed on the computer keyboard. The new arrival gave what would now become the norm, false answers. "Is there off street parking?" he needed to make security arrangements for the hoard.

"Yes Mr. Horder the suite comes with a double lock up garage one level down. Can I get someone to get your luggage?"

"No that's fine, if I could have the keys I'll put the car away and get organized."

The garage arrangement was perfect, each guest had a remote for the outer gate, and another button on the same hand piece controlled the roller door on the double garage. The whole area being the foundations of the building was an oversized concrete bunker.

As an extra precaution Emit switched the plug leads around on one bank of cylinders of the big car before packing $10,000-00 into his only suitcase.

"Emit who?" The new man said aloud as he walked into his new abode.

The entry was a small tiled section that opened into a formal lounge dining area. The furnishings were comfortable and expensive looking. Deep maroon bulky lounge suites, luxurious maroon curtains opened to picture the balcony with the beautiful Shoal Bay as the backdrop.

Sandy Horder, still holding his suitcase inspected both bedrooms and the kitchen. He checked inside cupboards, the built in robes and found what he was looking for in the toilet. Just the spot to hide $10,000-00 – a manhole.

He extracted five hundred dollars in notes and standing on the toilet seat lifted the lid on the manhole and stashed the bundles of notes into the ceiling. He then walked out onto the balcony and leaning on the railing quietly said, "Hello Sandy Horder." As he stood there he was filled with an overwhelming sense of freedom that he had never felt before.

Sandy knew he would never tire of the white sands and the steady lapping water of this paradise. He looked past the small waves to the boats pulling at their anchor ropes, and wondered how much some of those people found under the back seat of their car!

The next day Sandy applied for credit cards and opened accounts at six different banks and building societies, telling the same story each time. There would be $2,000-00 paid into the account each week in cash, that being the proceeds from rental properties.

The next step was to get a driver's licence in his new name this was a necessity if he was to have a new identity. Sandy Horder, resident of The Country Club Shoal Bay filled out all the forms at the local department office and was given the literature to study and a booking day for his test. That seemed to be all he had to do to start a new life.

The pale beer at the corner bar of the Country Club was to the new resident's liking, and he was on his second when a cheerful fellow, ten or twelve years his junior approached.

"How are ya, you're new."

"Yes." Sandy was taken aback but relished the company.

"You can always tell," the intruder pointed to the real estate brochure lying on the table, "you looking to buy or rent?"

"It's just a habit," the newcomer was guarded, "what about you?"

"Me, I live here it's the greatest place in the world."

Sandy smiled and nodded in agreement.

"A lot of the people who come here are from Melbourne," the younger man looked at Sandy. "You don't look like them. I'd say you're Sydney."

"Good observation," Sandy neither agreed nor disagreed, but the fellow had him laughing. He swallowed the last of his beer. "Can I buy you one?"

"Gotta get home for lunch, or the cook will go nuts."

As quick as he came, the welcomed intruder left.

"Jimmy, Jimmy," a fellow practicing a few shots on the pool table by himself called out holding up a cue. "A quick game's a good game."

"Tomarra," and with the nod of his head Sandy's new found friend was out the door in a flash.

It was several days before Sandy went back to the corner bar for a midday drink. He had been locked away in his apartment going through the road rules for his driving test. The licence was crucial. By the end of the third day he had virtually memorized the book. Exams were never his strong point, so Sandy just told himself he wasn't the old looser Emit, he was the successful Sandy. It worked, he got through. The lady on the counter almost apologized when she gave him the two P plates that he had to display while he was on his provisional licence. He in turn gave her that winner's smile.

With the newly acquired licence in his wallet, he was enjoying a beer at the corner bar when the cheerful fellow from a couple of days before walked in. He acknowledged several people as he counted out some change to the barman, took a good swallow from the glass, had a look around and then spotted Sandy and walked over as if on a mission.

"Did ya find a place yet?"

"Oh yes thank you," again Sandy was appreciative of the company, "I'm staying here."

"Oh you're staying here?" the younger man repeated as if that changed things. "Ya staying long?"

Sandy had intended to lay low as it were, and just blend in, so he told the truth. "I've booked in for a month."

At one of their meetings after a few weeks Jimmy asked "Ya like fishing?"

"I, ah, enjoy a day out." That wasn't the quite the truth as he had never fished before, but 'when in Rome.........' he thought to himself.

"You'll have to meet the big four."

"The what?"

"The big four, we meet every afternoon at the RSL Club."

"Sounds interesting, my name's Sandy Horder," he replied feeling a little puzzled and reaching across the table shook hands as the shorter man stood to reach.

"Jimmy Zininski."

"I think we had better have a beer Jimmy," Sandy reached for the other man's glass. "Tell me about this big four."

"Ah, just four blokes and me, we have a beer at the RSL as I said."

"Four blokes and you sound like the big five," Sandy said raising his glass, "here's the best."

"Yeah," Jimmy nodded, drank from his glass and said modestly. "They're four retired blokes, who like to drink and fish. Plenty of money," he added.

"That sounds like a good crew." Sandy then realized this was an acceptance of his new character. Emit Horsley would not have been invited to meet such a group.

"You gonna come?"

"Yes, I'll come and have a drink with you and your friends."

'Can't hurt,' Sandy thought and a good way to meet people.

All the time he had lived in the west no one ever asked him to join a new group or go to a football match. Emit probably looked as though he would have nothing to offer their company. Yet just sitting in this place, a stranger thinks Sandy would add something to their little group. Emit Horsley and Sandy Horder were so different and that could only be a good thing.

It was several weeks before Sandy decided to meet Jimmy's fishing friends.

"The RSL you say, when?"

"Four o'clock," Jimmy took his turn with the glasses.

"Are you retired Jimmy?"

"Yes, ah no," Jimmy answered then corrected himself, "I retired from work to come up here, now I do odd jobs and a bit of cleaning."

"And your friends? Are they in a similar situation?" Sandy asked.

"Ah hell no, they're genuine retirees old blokes finished work," Jimmy thought for a second, "Steve, he's a retired pilot, bit younger than the rest same thing though, plenty of money and no work."

CHAPTER 7

NEW FRIENDS

Sandy went to the RSL Club an hour before he was due to meet his new friends. The first thing that came to mind when his new mate Jimmy asked him to come to the Club for a drink was another identity fix, Club membership. While he was filling out the form, using his new licence for identity, he noticed two restaurants, a bistro, and the new gaming room. 'Gaming room' he thought. 'I can't keep cashing one hundred dollar notes at the hotel or the paper shop.' He walked over to the cashier's window and then mingled with players and stopped in front of a couple of machines, just like a holiday gambler looking for that lucky one.

It was a little after four when Sandy walked into the main bar area of the Club. Typical Club-land, stunning carpet that never seemed to mark and a big U shaped bar which was empty. The lunchtime crowd had gone and the evening surge was hours off.

The newcomer took it all in and spotted a table of men sitting by the windowed wall that showed another angle of Shoal Bay. He felt the security of the five $20 notes that he had just folded neatly and slipped into his shirt pocket as he headed towards his mark.

One of the men in the group turned away from the window to drink from his glass, looked up and spotted Sandy approaching. "How are you?" the man asked in a tone that would have embarrassed the naturally subdued Emit Horsley, but Emit didn't come into the Club that afternoon. The polished confident character of Sandy Horder answered for him feeling a little bit like a gate crasher.

"I'm fine," he hesitated and touched his breast pocket again "I'm to meet……"

"Hello mate, ah…" Jimmy Zininski looked around and tilted his head up. "Sandy! I'm sorry Sandy, let me get you a chair," he gave up his own seat and fetched another for himself. "Let me introduce you around."

Sandy shook hands around the table with this dubious lot. Jimmy hadn't mentioned that he was coming. "That's Jimmy," Dick Walker the retired Real Estate Agent said, "He can't keep two thoughts in that head of his at once."

The men would go on to meet every afternoon in the same spot and Sandy slotted right in. The transformation from the dominated Emit Horsley to the independent Sandy Horder took place as soon as the opportunity was presented. A new character was born the day Emit turned his car east away from Bulwer Street.

After the first couple of days the questions of a personal nature dropped off. The big four accepted Sandy for who he was, a quiet unassuming wealthy man. The boys discussed him in his absence a few times and tried to work out who he was.

Maurice Campbell the old farmer got a laugh when he related a short conversation he had had with Sandy in the men's room. "I said to him what did you do in your business Sandy? And he said 'I retired.'"

Walt McEnroe the ex-Motel owner said he had asked about Mrs. Horder.

"It didn't work out so we split the assets, he had said."

Sandy didn't elaborate on the fact that his domineering wife, mother of one, and mother's carer, got the run down house in Bulwer Street and he got the $10,000,000-00. The fact that Sandy was reluctant to discuss his past made him more affable and mystery only added to the myth that would surround him. To the last man the big four were glad this (newcomer) gentleman from the west chose their town for himself.

By the time Sandy had renewed his booking on the upstairs suite at the Country Club he had become a local. The lady who owned the coffee shop in the arcade up the street always had a chat to him when she poured the coffee just the way he liked it. The restaurateurs all knew him. He ate out all the time, and of course the big four knew everyone and everything that happened in the Bay.

Because he was a newcomer people told him things. He would take it all in and use snippets in his daily conversations. When his newspaperman told him that the landlord had given him notice that the building was to be sold at the end of his lease for redevelopment, Sandy advised him to talk to Col the Real Estate fellow on the corner. "I hear he's been offered a franchise and they are going to operate out of Nelson Bay. That corner site would make a great newsagency."

Sandy wisely summed things up before offering an opinion, and being objective never upset anybody. Really, anything that happened in the town didn't affect him one way or the other. His wealth gave him his independence and enviable life style.

The bar man at the Club was going off one afternoon about the Fisheries Department mailing out notices concerning the relocation of moorings on a popular cove. "I've moored boats on that same spot for twenty years," he told Sandy.

"Where are they moving you to?"

"I dunno."

"It might be a better spot."

His days were spent idly, morning coffee, reading the paper, midday drink at the corner bar, sometimes with Jimmy, and of course the four o'clock session at the RSL Club.

The good life started to show on the fifty eight year olds girth and he knew he needed more purpose in his life. He had noticed walkers from his balcony, mainly women in small groups briskly walking towards the heads each morning. Then seeing them come back an hour or an hour and a half later when he was having his morning coffee and reading his paper.

I need to do something like that, he thought. He looked at the shortbread biscuit and coffee, I don't need to do this. The next morning when he thought the last of the walkers had gone past the Country Club, Sandy came down the stairs wearing shorts, sweatshirt and joggers.

"Anyone for tennis," the girl on reception joked having never seen the house's most notable guest out of collared shirts and casual trousers.

"It's the diet next," Sandy replied "then I'll be dangerous."

In fifteen minutes he was almost to the heads and wondered where the walkers went from here. Two middle aged women came down a steep walking trail in front of him. "Hello Sandy."

"Hello," he replied not knowing them. "What's it like up there?" he looked up to the steep heavily grown headland.

"You won't get fit walking along the footpath," one of the ladies called out.

He walked into the thick of it and up. In minutes his heart rate was up from the idling speed it had been tuned to, and his body had lost a good glass full of fluid.

"Is there an exercise clinic or gymnasium in town Jimmy?" Sandy asked over a midday beer at the corner bar.

"Yeah there's one at the Club, why?"

"I might give that a go."

"What!" That's for old women and footballers."

Sandy laughed, Jimmy wasn't like others he said anything and he didn't have the money, but he still enjoyed the Bay and all its beauty just as they did, and the thing they were all here for was the fishing. "Are you ready for tomorrow," he changed the subject.

"Yes," Sandy replied, "that new gear came in for me yesterday." The new gear was fishing tackle.

"He's a good bloke that Rod, hey that's a good name for a fellow who owns a fishing gear shop," Jimmy laughed.

CHAPTER 8

SEA RESCUE

The sun made its presence felt when Maurice Campbell and Jimmy Zininski were doing the final preparations for their weekly day out. They had launched the *White Zephyr*, Maurice's sixteen foot runabout at the Shoal Bay boat ramp twenty minutes before. "You ice down the beer, I'll cut up some of this bait," old Maurice liked to give the younger man orders. "And don't touch any."

"Yes boss, no boss," Jimmy answered, he would have his first before they went out through the heads anyway.

Steve Flint strode along the jetty with his rod split over one shoulder and carrying a small tackle box.

"Here's Steve, good day Steve," Jimmy looked up from the ice box, "have you seen the others?"

"Walt and Dick were getting the papers, haven't seen Sandy."

"I hope he hasn't gone for his walk," Maurice called out not looking up from his cutting table.

"What's going on with Sandy and the walking routine?"

"I don't know Mavis saw him yesterday morning and couldn't wait to tell me when she got back," Maurice replied looking up again from his cutting duties, "reckons it would be good for all of us. I told her I've done my share of walking and bloody exercise around that farm for seventy years."

"You tell 'em you old bugger," Jimmy jumped in. It was in his nature to stir things up and keep it on the boil.

"What would you know you've never done any exercise in your bloody life, you sat in a little store room at the BHP all your life and did nothing?"

"And," the little ethnic fellow stalled, "got paid for it, you wouldn't catch me running around the hills of Scone with a stick in me hand chasing cows."

"Now boys," Steve timed his step onto the gently rocking boat, "it can't hurt him," being a bit of a diplomat, he patted Maurice on the belly. "It might get rid of that."

"You've been talking to Mavis" the older man accused.

A very shabbily dressed Dick Walker and the runner up in the gardening slash fishing clothes competition Walt McEnroe arrived on the scene.

"We're all here bar one," Dick was the outspoken one on everything, rightly pointed out.

"Sandy's gone for his walk he should be about half an hour," Jimmy turned up the heat under the pot.

"What the bloody hell's going on?" Dick looked to the sky for guidance.

"The old girl's on to me last night about going for a morning walk, all the wives are talking about him and he's never even met them!"

"I know, I know, I know," came the words of wisdom from the cutting board area.

"Maurice knows." Jimmy kept a straight face.

"You're right Dick," Walt dropped his bag onto the boat before carefully stepping over the gap, "the fellow at the IGA store told Yvonne that Sandy inquired about the healthy cooking classes held at the church hall in Nelson Bay!"

"And she suggested you might do the same?" Dick questioned.

"Along those lines."

"Here's Sandy!" Jimmy heralded the last arriver. The youngest of the crew admired the way this somewhat elusive newcomer kept everyone guessing with his sometimes subtle moves.

Sandy didn't have old fishing clothes. He wore the designer clothes he bought last month. Along with his new fishing gear he carried one clothing accessory the others didn't have, a raincoat.

"What's the coat for?" Dick who looked the exact opposite, apparel wise, asked.

"Be prepared Dick," Sandy smiled as he stepped on board.

The *White Zephyr* skimmed across perfect waters towards the heads, talk of exercise and wives tales was replaced with fishing tales and where to catch them this week. "The boys on the charter boat have been taking their customers to the wreck all week and having great success," Walt said. He liked to keep his eye on the catches and prices as he always did in business, and so spent a bit of time around the fishing co-operative, trawler boat owners and charter operators.

"What do you say we give that a go for an hour before we head up to the island?" Dick suggested.

Dick and Walt were closer than any of the others in the group. They lived in the same street and their backgrounds, both being business men gave them a lot in common.

"Why not?" Jimmy concurred taking his first from the esky.

"You've got seven left," Maurice said looking at him with a warning in his eye, beer rations were eight per man. The rest of the crew waited until the rods were put away. Not Jimmy anywhere anytime.

"I just want to get mine out of the way so as I can get on with the job I came here to do." Jimmy excused himself.

In an hour the five friends were spaced out around the boat, it was Maurice who jagged the first, a plate sized sea mullet, hooked behind the gills "Just lucky, we shouldn't have to pay that one." Even though Walt was the black money king of his time, and maybe because of it, he watched his dollars carefully. The payment he was referring to was the ten dollar boat fee each fisherman chipped in for the day out. First catch was excluded.

"Is that new gear of yours working for you Sandy?" Maurice called to the crew's newest member who sat alone on the bow.

"Works fine, just haven't caught a fish yet."

"The day's young, there's plenty of bait." The old man liked Sandy, he fitted in well, and he found his mystery alluring.

Just then the new rod bent, Sandy instinctively moved one hand up the rod and gave it a quick jerk, the load eased on the line then took up again.

"Got him!"

The fish did all the escape tricks it could, with its tail flash dance on top of the water and underneath, until eventually it succumbed to Sandy's steady hand on the rod.

"Well done," the old farmer congratulated as Sandy stood to wind the catch in.

"That deserves a drink," Steve looked at Jimmy.

"I'll shout,"

"You've got six left," the old farmer told the self-appointed waiter when he handed him his beer.

"You've got seven, I'll race you to the bottom," Jimmy didn't have a care in the world and it showed.

The crew on the *White Zephyr* unconsciously recognized their standing in relation to each other. It was the old time proven, age, position, money thing.

Maurice Campbell had the top job, there were no challengers. Besides his dominance in the age race, his working life had been a success in his wealth, his property holdings, and the recognition he had received in the innovative processes that he had been behind in revolutionizing his industry. Even now in retirement he sat on the board of the R.S.L. Club.

Dick Walker and his mate Walt McEnroe were a pair of self-made men in their respective careers. Like most in this category they looked on themselves as ground breakers. They did it with their ideas and hard work and they can back themselves up with money. Dick and Walt didn't have much time for life along the way it was all money and deals. Now they were retired they were going to have a good time no matter what.

Steve Flint the ex-pilot could see only a well-paid time span in Dick and Walt's working life. He enjoyed their company but felt entirely satisfied with his own achievements and didn't need to prove anything. As a boy he dreamed of joining the air force, which he did. He wasn't a fighter pilot but flew just about everything else that the RAAF had, and he did some of that on active service. He and his lovely wife Lyn enjoyed an enviable life style in their beach front unit supported by three retirement funds. They had no children and put a lot of thought into their concessionary air fares, complements of the Qantas superannuation fund.

Steve acknowledged Maurice as the no nonsense man who would have made it in any field. If there was one person in the group Steve was fully at ease with, it was Jimmy.

Jimmy Zininski had no pretenses he thanked God every morning he woke up in this paradise. He had little savings and little need for them. His redundancy payout had been rolled over into a managed fund, this was then enhanced with his early morning cleaning job at the Club and the handy man jobs he was famous for, 'it's always cheaper if ya pay cash.' With no mortgage Jimmy and wife Isa had the disposable income for a comfortable waterside retirement. Jimmy and his wife were not social types, they didn't dine out. Isa helped her husband with his cleaning job at the Club each morning, doing the lot herself when he went out fishing. She was a homely woman who loved to cook. Her best days were when one of the children would ring to say that they were coming up for the weekend. All the socializing done in the Zininski family was done by her husband.

While the youngest member of the group looked on Maurice as a fatherly figure, the other three could change rankings daily in his opinion. Sandy was graded highest with

Jimmy because he didn't say anything about himself, his past was in the past, but the man had it all.

It was just after eleven o'clock when the Skipper remarked about the gathering rain clouds beyond the island. "We'll give it another ten minutes boys and then we'll pull them in."

Sandy had been watching the horizon for some time. He looked south and wet his finger. It was an old boy scout's trick but a reliable one. He wouldn't leave it any longer.

Dick had been catching a few and the boys weren't eager to pull their lines in.

Walt baited up again and cast out. His mate not to be outdone had another try.

It was a quarter of an hour before Maurice called full time. "Come on boys those clouds are getting closer." Walt had one more throw, Sandy could feel the slight breeze from the south on his face and the negligible swell starting to lap the hull.

It was another five minutes before Maurice stood in his spot behind the wheel and twisted the key, there was an unfamiliar clunk. Maurice tried again, same noise and not the one he wanted to hear. He turned to look at the big twin Mercury outboards and tried again this time holding the key on, the same noise multiplied. Sandy stood up "Are they in series?"

Everyone looked at Maurice who had no answer. Sandy unclipped the top of the motor closest to him and lifted the lid. "Yes they are, no auxiliary," he answered his own question quietly and thoughtfully, Jimmy was immediately at his side.

"What's wrong?"

"Starter motor," he slipped his hand down inside the motor casing and felt the end of the small shaft, "I might be able to get a spanner on to that."

Nobody said anything. In the quiet, the lapping on the hull was noticeable, the clouds were now ominous.

Maurice knelt along-side the other two with a small red metal tool box he had grabbed from the cupboard under the wheel. Sandy masterly chose the right spanner and going by feel was able to get it onto the end of the shaft. All eyes were on the man who had their fate in his hands. The crew watched the expression on Sandy's face as he lifted the load carefully with force and felt the shaft free up. "Try that Maurice."

The old man put one hand on the motor and one on his knee and pushed himself up. He didn't look at the clouds, he just hoped against hope. One twist of the key and the two big Mercuries fired up. Maurice tried to steady himself and pulled the wheel as he fell. Sandy leaped from his position at the rear of the boat but couldn't save the old man as he hit the deck heavily, as he turned Maurice over he could see a slight cut on his forehead.

"Is he on medication?"

"Yes, insulin," Steve Flint answered. "A bit of a shock can set that off."

Sandy went through the old man's pockets and found a small clear bottle. He looked up, Steve was using his first aid know how to check the patient's heart and breathing.

"Will you get a cup of water please Jimmy?" Sandy asked. "Then take the wheel and head in."

Maurice was embarrassed as he sat on the port side for the ride back in. "I don't know what happened," he said feeling the band aid on his forehead.

"It happens to me all the time after a few drinks," Jimmy made light of it from his spot behind the wheel.

The old man put his hand on the back of the aluminium bench seat to get up.

"I'll take her in Jimmy," after all he was the Skipper.

"Why don't you sit back, I'll take her in," said Steve who was considered to be the natural choice.

Sandy had been watching that front and estimated that they would encounter some weather before they docked. He kept his eyes on Steve closely and at that point realized he would one day own a boat of his own.

The *White Zephyr* was a good forty minutes from the heads when the rain hit. Sandy buttoned up his coat and bumped the power lever forward a couple of notches. "Is everything alright up there?" Maurice called from up in the bow where he and three of the four other fishermen had now taken shelter.

"Yep," Sandy answered his eyes peering through the side Perspex.

"We're right on course," Steve assured Sandy, he liked to sit up with the Captain, the tracker and the navigation screen were his forte.

"I've been watching that runabout over here on the right for a few minutes," Sandy said concerned. "They'd be doing it tough." The White Zephyr raised her bow and crashed through a few as the swell heightened. The runabout bounced as she maintained her speed, as if they wanted to keep up. Steve picked up the radio handset and rattled off a location message to make contact with the runabout. He lifted his finger from the device and awaited a reply.

"Yeah thanks White Zephyr," a voice crackled through the speaker, "it's bloody rough we'll try and maintain this speed and visual contact, we recon we're over a half an hour from the heads."

"E.T.A. is right, will maintain visuals, out." Steve kept it formal.

"What's going on?" Maurice ducked his head out from the bow section bracing himself as he looked up.

"Just made contact with the other boat, they're going to follow us in." Steve answered.

"It's getting rough. We're about a half an hour out?" Maurice questioned. The bow of the sixteen footer boat was lifted out of the water suddenly by a cunning wave that had the old man grappling for support.

"You stay down there Maurice we're right up here." Sandy advised, assuming the leadership role vacated by the older man.

"And keep those pills handy," Steve said in a voice that couldn't be heard. He braced himself for a wave and looked out at a sky and sea that blended together in a fierce colour of grey.

The runabout took a big hit broadside that left her motionless. The two occupants Muscat Farincini and his accomplice Dominic Lotenzo were panic stricken.

"They're in trouble," Sandy said turning across a wave in his bid to assist. The three men came out through the open hatch when the boat turned, shielding themselves from the now side on watery onslaught.

"What's going on?" Dick now showed his weak side in the panicked look on his face.

"You three get back up in the bow, Jimmy you stay here." Sandy didn't take his eyes off the little runabout, but to be paralysed in this sea could be disastrous. "Jimmy hang on to something, make sure that rope's attached and throw it when I tell you," Sandy pointed to a loose rope and tried to manoeuvre the *White Zephyr* with the waves now lifting it from the rear.

Dominic was shouting and making all sorts of hand signals to them. "We're doing our bloody best mate," Sandy said as he edged within throwing distance for Jimmy to do his thing.

"There's a bloke in the water," Jimmy yelled and identified somebody struggling wildly. The *White Zephyr* was on a collision course with the runabout as they came down a wave. Sandy spotted someone in the water in the ravine beside the stricken boat. He pulled a lifebuoy off the headboard next to the wheel and passed it to Steve.

"When we get close drop this over him," Sandy indicated to the man in the water. "Jimmy throw the rope........now," he yelled over the threatening noises of Mother Nature.

With one hand on the power and an eye to the rear, Sandy judged it right as he powered away from the lifting wave for a second and positioned between the drowning man in the water and the crippled craft.

"Get him Steve, and then give him a rope." As Sandy turned the *White Zephyr* to face the onslaught of the sea he fired orders to his deckhands. "Jimmy, lift the rope we're coming under it. Steve get that rope to the fisherman and start pulling him in." And to the fellow in the disabled runabout who couldn't hear him anyway. "Hang on."

Within a minute Steve had the fisherman who was in the water at the side of the boat but couldn't get his huge twenty odd stone frame over the side of their boat. A wave crashed over the bow of the smaller boat and sweeping along the side almost took the exhausted man from Steve's grasp.

Sandy looked at Muscat's pleading eyes and let the wheel go. He fought to release his desperate grip on the gunnel and with a double wrist grip Sandy took a suicide stand up on the top edge and reefed the exhausted man in.

With no one at the wheel the boat lurched sideways on a wave and threatened to roll it over. Jimmy jumped over a sliding esky, grabbed the wheel and turned the boat back into the wave. The switch in direction and the rising of the bow suddenly spilled the two remaining men out of their shelter in the forward section and sprawled them together with Sandy, Steve and the exhausted fisherman into each other on the slippery washed deck.

Sandy was soon back at the wheel issuing orders.

"Good work Jimmy, you go back and give Steve a hand and keep an eye on the tow." He looked at the others. "You blokes might be better back up in the front we're not out of this yet." Nobody argued or asked why.

Wave after wave tormented the fishermen as the sea worsened. Jimmy had two ropes on the tow to ease the strain. Steve comforted the half drowned fisherman who was now bringing up buckets of salt water and other unpleasant gut dregs. "You'll be right mate," words that were meant for comfort were given without much conviction.

"Maurice has had another turn," Dick was at the bow hatch more panicked than before.

"Give him another pill," Sandy ordered.

"Is that advisable?" Dick questioned.

"Read the instructions and give him one anyway," Sandy said not taking his intense stare from the way ahead, "it's all we've got."

Sandy looked back at the two big Mercury outboards churning the sea behind them and the little runabout bouncing from side to side on the end of its leash.

"Double up that tow Jimmy," Sandy shouted.

"I've already doubled it."

"Do it again."

Jimmy wouldn't argue or ask why. Sandy was now in charge.

Steve looked up from the deck where he sat with the rescued fisherman left in his care and then at Sandy who seemed to revel in each challenge that was thrown at him. The fisherman looked at the stranger at the wheel through dazed eyes, he owed him his life.

Up in the bow Maurice and Walt felt every deafening bang as the front of the *White Zephyr* crashed through every wave. "Will we ever get out of this?" Maurice asked after he came to with the help of his medication.

"Sandy's got everything under control. He just dragged someone out of the ocean" Walt answered with complete confidence.

"In this?" The old skipper asked.

"Where's Dick?"

Dick allowed fear to beat determination. He hung on to the port side chrome railing with his head over the side. When he had no more to bring up he didn't really care if a wave swept him off to who knows where. As he straightened up a crashing wave knocked his weakened body off balance and sent it clambering down the slippery deck to the rear of the boat. More out of embarrassment Dick struggled to get his footing on the perilous deck and slipped over the back narrowly missing the two propellers, Jimmy saw the runabout hit him hard.

"Sandy" it was a desperate cry.

Sandy had sensed a catastrophe before he spun around. In a split second he spotted Dick going under behind their tow. With a huge hit of adrenalin and a burst of energy he tore off his coat and with a long dive from the chrome railing he found himself only a few strokes from Dick. Jimmy was back at the wheel steering them again away from their destination.

Dominic, in the little tow was able to get a rope to the two in the water and started pulling them in as Jimmy bought their boat around. All on board the *White Zephyr* watched helplessly as Sandy struggled to push the unconscious body of Dick Walker into the runabout. He used his last drop of energy to scramble over the back of the small craft himself. He looked at Jimmy and pointed towards home.

Once he assured himself that Dick was alright at the back of the small runabout Sandy gingerly edged his way over to Dominic who hung on desperately to the tall stem of one of the seats. "Can you hook me up to our boat on that radio?"

"Yes, there's someone on there," he said whilst not letting go of his vice like grip on the chair stem, "just press the bloody button to speak."

Sandy reached up and grabbed the bottom of the wheel and pulled himself up.

"Tow craft, tow craft come in, over," it was Steve's voice.

"Yeah I got you Steve."

"You've got to cut back on the speed, we're barely hanging on."

"OK how are you and Dick?"

"We'll make it." At no time did Sandy ever give up.

Sandy dragged Dick to the forward section of the boat for shelter and tied him to the other seat stem. There was no way this weak man could otherwise hang on.

"What if she goes over?"

"She won't go over."

"What about you?" Dominic asked.

"I've got to see what's going on."

As Sandy pulled the rope to tighten the knot he reached up to grab the bottom of the wheel and at that precise time a mountain of a wave lifted the little boat vertically. Dominic swung out like a trapeze artist his feet not touching the deck. Dick dangled in mid-air by the rope Sandy had just secured around him.

Before they knew what had happened, the tow pulled them down the back of the wave. Everything happened in reverse with Sandy now crashing back up under the wheel again. With his remaining strength, Sandy grabbed Dominic, his friend Dick and the three of them lay on the deck jammed into the space between the two tall seats and the control headboard. They said nothing, they kept their heads down. They waited.

More than once the small craft went vertical on this frightening trip back to port. It was the tow, which was now down to two ropes that kept pulling them down. 'We were a half an hour out a half an hour ago' Sandy thought, 'when will this end?' He dare not move or release his wrestler's grip on the other two.

Back on the *White Zephyr,* Jimmy stood behind the wheel of the larger craft with Steve at his side constantly watching the screen. They could see nothing past the bow but waves and sheets of rain. Three or four times Steve gave Jimmy a nudge. "Turn back up towards your right."

The sea was driving them south past the entrance. This was taking up time and Steve knew, with the motors working so hard, they were using up valuable fuel. He didn't say anything but noticed that they had used up half of the remaining fuel since he and Jimmy had taken over from Sandy.

The same thoughts went through Sandy's mind lying on the deck of the tow. He recalled checking the gauge when he first spotted the runabout and it was down to over a quarter of a tank which was right as they were more than three quarters of the way through their trip. But this heavy going and the tow would use up more than normal. They moved at a snail's pace but the motors were working hard. With no forward motion they wouldn't last long out here. Both Sandy and Steve were worried. We must be nearly there Sandy thought.

Steve looked at the screen then into the grey blank curtain hoping to see something to relate to their position. There was nothing. He looked back at the screen that showed them being pushed off their course again. He grabbed Jimmy's shoulder again. "Back up," he pointed and shouted above the roar. Steve checked the fuel gauge yet again. 'Even if we were in the bay by now I doubt if we would have enough fuel to make it to the dock,' he thought.

"Look" Jimmy yelled and spun the big wheel further back up, some miraculous break allowed the men to see the coast line, there was no opening but they were back.

"It's got to be just up there," Steve pointed right where Jimmy had turned.

The big boat rocked as she took the waves side on while the smaller craft obediently followed with long lifts along the face of the waves and long drops down the back. In minutes the screen showed Steve what he had been sweating on, a break in the line. "That's it Jimmy, keep her in the middle."

The cheeky little Pole went from deckhand to Skipper in the next two minutes. Waves were crashing five and six meters high on either side of the heads and splashing back over their boat. The onslaught of water out of the normally placid playground of the bay could be likened to a dam bursting up stream. It seemed everything was against them finding safety.

Jimmy leaned on the power leaver and pushed it all the way forward. He ploughed through the onslaught at The Heads until he felt the boat pick up speed away from the mess in its wake and into more stable waters of the bay. The youngest and now a proven champion of the crew looked back at the tow still bouncing on the waves of the bay and knocked half the speed off, they had made it. Although he couldn't see his destination Jimmy turned towards Shoal Bay.

Away from The Heads, the waters, still raw for paradise, subsided some. Visibility was extended far beyond the bow allowing Jimmy and Steve to breath of sigh of relief.

Walt sheepishly poked his head through the hatch from the bow section and saw Steve and Jimmy leaning over the forward head board, The Heads behind them. "We made it," he announced.

Maurice followed, holding both sides of the opening. He looked about, as if to make sure, the waters had momentarily placated.

"Where's Sandy?" he hesitated "and Dick?"

"In the tow," Jimmy lifted his head. He was relieved it was over.

"How?" Walt now questioned.

"Oh man," Steve the normally cool one of the group, was giving in to exhaustion and emotions. "Dick was washed overboard, Sandy went in after him."

"What out there?" the old man asked and pointed.

"Flew off the rail," Steve stood up and mimicked the dive with his right arm.

"Waves were twice as high as the boat."

"Good grief!" Maurice used the strongest words he had left in him.

"The man deserves a medal," Steve commended.

"And what about him?" Maurice gestured to the sick, drenched man as big as a whale now sitting up at the back of their boat.

"Gee I forgot all about him," Steve said turning around, "we had better radio in and have an ambulance waiting."

Muscat, who was at the back of the boat now owed these fishermen, heard the conversation and lifted his hand and shook his head. Without talking he indicated he wanted no more fuss

Steve picked up the hand set, their only link with the tow. Sandy was already there. "Well done boys."

"What about you fellows, do you need an ambulance waiting for when we get in?"

"No we're alright, just swallowed a bit of water that's all."

If Dick Walker could add to the conversation he wouldn't agree, so he just lay on the floor of the tow trying to think of more pleasant places.

When the boys on the White Zephyr first spotted the jetty at Shoal Bay another fishing boat of equal dimensions occupied the end spot, the best place to unload. As they got closer the other boat moved off to make way. Maurice, who was now at the helm deemed this a gentlemanly gesture and acknowledge with a blast on the air horns.

Eight or ten people, some off the previous boat, gathered at the end of the jetty seemingly anxious. Two fellows caught the docking ropes and pulled the *White Zephyr* in. When the motors were finally silenced one of the group who had secured the bow rope called out to Maurice who he knew casually as a recreational fisherman. "You blokes had a rough time out there."

"Yes," Maurice stepped onto the wharf first with Steve by his side: the old man still wasn't one hundred percent.

"You had a person in the water is everything alright?"

Steve looked at the man questioningly.

"Mate we could hear your transmissions, couldn't get through to you on the radio and couldn't find you. The Water Police and two of the fleet are out there now looking for you."

"We had to come in," his mate interjected, "it was too big for us. What happened to the bloke in the water?" he asked.

"Which one? We had two in there!" Jimmy called from the boat as he tried to help their passenger to his feet.

"What!" he exclaimed as he jumped up to help.

"Thanks mate, they'll need a hand back there as well," Jimmy accepted indicating to Sandy standing up in the tow who by now had a rope over a pylon.

Two of the onlookers scrambled to secure the second boat.

"You had two blokes in the water," one of the crew from the first boat looked at Steve Flint unbelievingly. "Out there in that!?"

A stocky fellow in a weathered hat with a face to match looked at Jimmy.

"What happened to the other one?"

"He's back there," Jimmy answered and pointed to the tow.

Fishermen and miners have a common thread in their fabric makeup, where rewards are sometimes shrouded with danger. This bonds them like no other groups of men. The fishermen on the jetty broke into two teams, one to each boat. "Let's have a look at these blokes," one took charge, "they're going to need medical help."

"No mate," their newly acquired passenger spoke for the first time still supported by Jimmy as he attempted to step up on the gunnel. "If I can just get onto some steady ground and something warming for the inside I'll be right."

Miraculously a small brown flask went through a couple of sets of hands to the survivor. He held the bottle up as a toast. "Which one is Sandy?" he asked humbly.

The crew of the *White Zephyr* looked at the tow where the man stood, the eyes of everyone on the dock followed, not knowing why. "Thank you my man," he then raised the flask above his head then put it to his lips.

In ten minutes the jetty in Shoal Bay seemed to be the place to be. A case of a crowd attracting a crowd, everyone wanted to see the men saved from the ocean and the hero responsible. Sandy the unwilling protagonist felt better as Sandy in the background when he tapped Maurice, who was enjoying telling his part of the sea adventure, on the shoulder.

"I'm going to slip off. I'll see you all this afternoon at the Club."

"Hey you can't go, the boys at the Fishing Club will want to talk to you," the other Captain said disappointingly, "A report will have to be made out."

"Maurice is going to look after that," the reluctant hero answered.

"I'm with you," Muscat said as he shrugged off the borrowed blanket someone had put around his shoulders. His mate was also keen to get out of the spotlight. Before anyone could say 'what's going on' the three main characters in the in the great sea rescue had left the scene.

Just out of the glare of the wondering crowd Muscat stopped Sandy with his outstretched hand. "Man I haven't had a chance to thank you." Sandy Horder looked into the same pleading dark eyes that he saw standing on the gunnel of the *White Zephyr* a couple of hours ago. Muscat was of Italian descent in his mid-fifties and unhealthily overweight. His greasy tight curly hair was a mess of back and silver, his skin swarthy, a couple of days facial hair made him look unsavoury.

Sandy took his hand somewhat questioningly as he still wondered what these fellows were doing out in the open sea in such a small boat without any fishing gear. "Muscat Farincini," shook Sandy's hand vigorously introducing himself. "Dominic Lotenzo," he continued introducing his companion.

Sandy shifted his gaze and his thoughts to the other man. He definitely came from the same region as the one doing all the talking. Swarthy skin, tight curly black hair, unshaven face but a well cultivated moustache on his top lip. He was probably ten years younger than his friend and unlike his comrade under his soaked tee shirt he had a well-toned body.

He wasn't eager to talk but smiled and nodded when Sandy took his hand.

"Man you saved my life, your mate couldn't get me in that boat, it was too high and I was too heavy. You shoudda seen him Dominic," the fat man looked to his mate, "he pushed his friend outta the way grabbed me wrist and just pulled me over the side, I thought me arm was gonna come off."

"Glad to be of help," Sandy genuinely wanted to get back to his suite at the Country Club he had felt for his wallet just before they docked and realized it was missing. If it was at the bottom of the ocean it could cause a problem, besides credit cards and licence which were his new identity there was a list of bank accounts, credit unions, and building societies that he relied on to do his daily chores, the chores that legitimated the Sandy Horder conglomerate.

"Let's go have a drink," Muscat suggested.

"Look I can't go now I really have something I must do," Sandy held up his hands and shook his head.

"Man we gotta get together, I owe you me life." His newly acquired admirer was feeling better by the second and he wanted to celebrate with his new found friend.

"There's a good Italian restaurant up behind the main street in Nelson Bay, we give you a good night."

"Yes I know it," Sandy replied.

"What's your name?" Muscat was smiling.

"Sandy Horder."

"OK Sandy Horder seven o'clock tonight."

Sandy went straight across the road to the Country Club and used the side entrance which was popular with guests straight from the pool or the beach. He nodded and smiled at the receptionist, not wanting to get into a conversation. "Mr. Horder what's going on, there was a boat in trouble we heard it was you."

"Everything's fine," Sandy brushed it off and accepted his key.

"But all those people on the jetty," the young receptionist wanted to know.

"A big catch maybe," he replied as he headed for the door, he had to make sure his wallet was secure.

Once upstairs he unlocked the door and hurried to the bedroom. The maid had been, everything was tidy and the curtains were opened. He pulled open the second drawer in a solid timber chest and pushed his hand to the back, there was the familiar shape of his wallet. Sandy breathed a sigh of relief, he sat back on the bed, in the life he had manufactured he couldn't make mistakes, one inquiring question in setting up these bank accounts again could unmask Sandy Horder.

He thought about the girl on the front desk and what had happened out there today, people may start to ask questions.

Right on seven o'clock Sandy got out of a cab in front of the Pasta 'n Seafood. "How about I give you a call in a couple of hours Jeff," he told the cab driver.

"If it's after ten you'll get Shirley, I'll be going to the Club."

"This won't take that long."

He closed the cab door and looked both ways on the near deserted street. It was a welcomed respite from the commotion at the R.S.L. Club earlier in the afternoon, everybody wanted to hear about the rescue. Sandy, who didn't want his identity on display for obvious reasons, slipped away and left the talking to the big four. This was never going to be a good idea, the story only got bigger and now better thanks to the reluctant hero.

When he got back that afternoon to the Country Club the receptionist couldn't wait to tell their famous guest that the guy from The Port Stephens Examiner had been in looking for him. "Gee sorry I missed him." Sandy said unconvincingly.

The Pasta 'n Seafood was only about a dozen tables, and nine of these were awaiting their guests, Sandy's two new friends were sipping on the house red at the back corner. "Hi boys," he said as he approached their table.

"Sandy," Muscat called out as he stood up flashing a welcoming smile that he never had when they first met that morning. He was now cleanly shaven and wore a crisp white shirt with the top three buttons undone displaying an abundance of body hair on a big chest. His mass of thick curly hair had been slicked down. He had obviously gone to the trouble to show his refined side as a contrast to the image depicted earlier in the day. "Take a load off your feet," he said while still gripping Sandy's hand firmly. "Have a glass of wine?"

Sandy looked at the carafe of red on the table and remembered sipping from casks of red sitting in his shed back in Bulwer Street and the sick mornings that followed. "I might try a beer thanks."

Muscat caught the waitress's eye, ordered the beer and poured himself and his mate Dominic two generous servings from the carafe.

"Here's to you Sandy Horder, I owe you my life."

"Cheers," Sandy said as he raised his glass to acknowledge the thanks.

"Tell me my friend, you don't seem to wear the hero saving bloke thing real well, Dominic here and I," he pointed to his friend, "both said you wanted to get away from that mob on the wharf real quick like this morning."

"Yes well," Sandy hesitated wondering what these fellows were getting at. "I had something pressing that had to be done."

"Yeah well we have something pressing that has to be done too," Muscat Farincini did all the talking his friend never took his eyes off Sandy as if looking for some fault. "We aren't looking to get in the papers the same as we don't think you are." His grammar was jumbled but he had picked Sandy in one. "So we'll take you into our confidence." The fat man leaned forward. "No," he changed his mind. "Let's order tea first."

Muscat Farincini was fifty three years old, an opportunist with a friendly nature and a positive attitude. He read his stars regularly and the planets were always in line, even if they weren't. Here was an amicable Italian who knew the world was his oyster, life was full of highs for this man. The lows, and there had been some were seen as taking the wrong fork in the path of life. Get back on track get the new venture going.

Take for instance the time when the Banks took back his four motor dealerships on Sydney's north shore to clean up the mess that was created when he and a 'mate' were building the biggest apartment block on the Northern Beaches. Half way through the project Muscat bought four of the surrounding properties and submitted new plans to make the venture twice as big. Litigation, community objections, council dormancy all playing against and rising interest rates stopped the job. That wasn't a low, he came out of it alright, he was not bankrupt, and he squared the books.

Then there was Pet Parlour Glamour World. A place where ladies could bring their precious four legged companions for a shampoo and a brush, while enjoying health drinks, a massage or the exercise circuit. They sprung up all over Sydney under a franchise plan. It should have worked, but good natured Muscat didn't screen the franchise applicants very thoroughly, and wasn't all that particular on training. The fact that he kept half the sites for himself also wasn't good business sense. The Banks moved again. In the wash up, in the middle of a real estate boom, the Italian entrepreneur was again able to square the books. He tried and came out debt free once again.

His lack of education and mastering of the English language aside, we all know what he meant. And what it meant roughly translated was "Nothing ventured, nothing gained." In for a penny, in for a pound. No guts no glory. One door closes etc. It was after the failure of the pet business that Muscat moved to sunny Queensland.

"Let us show you how the Italians eat seafood my friend," Muscat summoned the waitress.

"Can we have three servings of the squid, with a small dish of olive oil and garlic bread?" he asked, "another carafe of your beautiful red wine, another beer for my friend here. And in fifteen minutes," the big Italian said slowly "bring out the lobster with separate side salad, Italian dressing." He rubbed his chin completely satisfied with his own choice while Dominic played the servant with the wine.

"So you and your mates are big fishermen," now continually smiling Muscat stated as he leaned back in his chair about to sip on the big goblet of red wine.

"Yes recreational," Sandy poured the remainder of the beer into his glass not mentioning that this morning was his first try at fishing on the high seas.

"Funny place the ocean. Can change just like that," the Italian clicked his fingers.

"You might need a bigger boat next time you go out," Sandy advised.

"Yeah, I hired that one yesterday from the bloke at the Marina; he said I shouldn't go outside in it."

"Have you taken it back to him?" Sandy asked knowing that the Marina was quite a way from the Shoal Bay jetty.

"No I told him to go and get it, gee if it wasn't for you blokes he wouldn't have a boat at all." The Italian laughed.

Sandy smiled thoughtfully as he put his glass back on the table.

"Did you catch any fish?" He asked knowing there was no gear on the boat.

"We weren't looking for fish."

"Muscat," Dominic spoke at last.

The big man looked sideways at his friend.

"The food's coming."

The conversation was put on hold while plates were handed around.

The big man joined his hands and looked up, "We thank you God…"

Sandy sat silently shocked as he watched Dominic join his hands and bowed his head.

"OK let's eat," the big man said as if the formalities were over.

After a second mouthful their guest broke the silence.

"What were you two fellows looking for?"

Muscat chewed on the rubbery squid then broke off a piece of garlic bread.

"There's a boat under the water out there," he looked at Dominic for approval. His companion nodded and went back for more of the bread. These men were here to eat as well as talk.

Sandy Horder knew when to listen and when not to show his hand. The silence was deafening. Muscat picked another piece of squid from his plate and kept his eyes low, thoughtfully trying to select the right words. "Me and Dominic here, we worked in Queensland for a couple years. We got to know lots of people, mainly our countrymen. They was involved in the import business."

"I see." Sandy looked around as if he could be sprung in the company of a couple of crooks.

"No it's not like you think, they imported boats, big luxury cruisers from Hong Kong, sailed them down to the Gold Coast and Sydney."

"And?"

"There's one of them sitting on the ocean floor out where you saw us today."

"How long has it been there?"

"1997."

"Wouldn't be much good now."

"No, the boat probably wouldn't be, but what's on it would."

"Hey listen boys," Sandy put down his fork, "I was glad we were able to help you today but I don't want to hear about anything illegal."

"Who said anything was illegal," the big Italian looked his guest right in the eye he had gone this far, he had to tell the rest of the story. He looked again at his friend. And so the story began.

"Just before Hong Kong went independent in 1997 the big boys started getting their stuff out. Some things they didn't want to go through customs, they sold their properties and bought big boats up to eighty foot and filled them with loot. Now loot is not bad stuff," the Italian explained.

"They turned their assets into cash and bought easily transportable stuff like precious gems, silver and gold. They slipped it on their big cruisers and got it out."

"Why are you telling me this, I could be a cop?" It all sounded a bit far-fetched to Sandy. These two fellows out in the ocean in a little boat looking for sunken treasure!

"Why are we telling you, and I don't care if you are a cop, I am telling you because you saved my life, our lives," Muscat corrected himself and leaned across the table to put his hand on Sandy's shoulder.

"You are now part of my family what's ours is yours, my friend."

"I appreciate your nice words Muscat," Sandy used the man's name for the first time, and found trust and respect.

"It's not just me and Dominic my friend, everybody would have drowned out there today if it wasn't for you," he went on "and the bloke who went over the back of the boat he would have been first to die, he wouldn't last a half a minute without you."

"We all got back," Sandy didn't want any more kudos.

"You won't get away that easily my friend, a lotta people are talking about it. The papers will want to talk to you."

The reluctant hero, with his obscure background realized as soon as he changed his identity his character had changed. He knew this was his second chance at life. Why it happened, he didn't know and couldn't justify. He was so comfortable in his new life. This he knew was where he was supposed to be.

The men talked, ate and drank for a couple of hours. Muscat had asked Sandy why he shied away from the publicity that would come no matter what.

"I came to this place for a new start, I broke away from my other life," was his only explanation.

"It's your business my friend, if I can help just ask."

"You're not on the run?" Dominic didn't say a lot and when he did it came out wrong.

"Hey!" the big man slapped the table.

Sandy smiled.

"That boat of yours," Muscat joined his hands on the table and looked at his guest.

"It would have some kind of fish finding underwater device?"

"Well it's not my boat, it belongs to Maurice the older fellow, but it does have a screen and a sounding instrument."

"You're not a fisherman are you?"

"No."

"I suppose you are going to tell me now you're not much of a swimmer either."

Sandy liked this Italian, he was like an old friend that he'd linked up with after a long period and they picked up where they left off, where in fact he'd only met him today.

"We find strengths and abilities when others are in need." Sandy was surprised at his own words when he noticed the big Italian raise an eyebrow.

"Well said my friend, keep that one for the papers tomorrow."

"Tell me how do you know where this boat is out there under the water?" Sandy changed the subject. He was still a non-believer.

"Well there was three cruisers come out of Hong Kong the last week of November in ninety seven," the Italian dialect on the English language was colourfully matched with table illustrations using the salt pepper and sugar utensils "all headed for Sydney. They was loaded, now these two," Muscat moved the salt and pepper shakers away from his plate towards Sandy's.

"They was hit by pirates two days out of port."

"Pirates?" Sandy leaned forward and kept his surprised voice low.

"M-a-t-e," the Italian shook his head. "You don't know, they lay in wait, they can smell the loot, when they find you. You're gone. They take everything sink the boat no one left to tell the tale.

Sandy sat up straight and wiped his mouth with the napkin. If he was taking a bit of convincing about the sunken treasure off the coast, this colossal tale now of luxury cruisers, loot and pirates was either that, or it was all true.

"Mate you never heard about this before?" The big Italian questioned tilting his head and leaning across the table.

Sandy had lost his appetite, he wanted to hear more.

"Mate," he used the slang as a persuading tool, "you don't know the type of money I'm talking about here, these, these, financiers, dealmakers call them what you want," the man waved his hands around as if grabbing the words out of the air. He leaned forward. He couldn't paint a bigger picture. "They move hundreds of millions of dollars, in the biggest most flamboyant way, they send their exotic furniture, Lamborghinis and Persian rugs stuffed with American dollars in shipping containers, but the stuff," Muscat rubbed his thumb and forefinger together, "they don't want customs to see what comes in on the cruiser."

The Italian brushed the salt and pepper shakers away and positioned the sugar bowl to the side of Sandy's plate. "This one, the biggest of the three, eighty foot, two huge industrial Volvos converted to marine she was fast, she had to get through, special cargo."

Sandy didn't ask about the special cargo as the narrator had expected but instead referred to his original question. "So how do you know where this boat is?"

"Well the Captain, one of our countrymen who was hired to bring the big boat down was able to out run the pirates by staying out further and taking longer than a boat that size normally would."

"Very interesting," Sandy said moving the sugar bowl towards his plate thoughtfully.

"The big boat with special cargo moves in close to the coast and sinks off Port Stephens. Well there is a change of plans, the big boys, here in Sydney think the Indonesian pirates, know what's on board and decide to off load everything in Port Stephens and take it the rest of the way by road. I told you they were Indonesian pirates didn't I?"

"Special cargo" Sandy reiterated.

It was now Muscat who side stepped the special cargo issue.

"Our country man radioed a mayday call early that evening and gave an exact position and then nothing."

"What do you mean nothing?"

"The coast guard responded straight away with boats and planes and found nothing. No boat no wreckage, nothing."

"Maybe the Captain skipped with the special cargo." As he said it Sandy knew that the obvious answer wasn't the right one.

"Where do you hide an eighty foot cruiser in a coupla hours? Na" the big Italian looked at Sandy and tapped the table with his forefinger, "she's sittin' on the bottom."

"A big boat like that could sit out a storm you'd think."

"The weather report shows there was a storm that night but the mayday call didn't mention that, the official report said that it was a panicked call giving only time and position."

Sandy sat quiet in thought. This was good dinner conversation an adventurous riddle.

"And what do you think?" It was Dominic's turn; he caught Sandy's attention when he pointed to the ceiling.

"Oh no," Sandy laughed.

"I've read up on it, a lotta stuff goes unexplained," Muscat leaned forward his elbows on the table.

Sandy bought another round as was his habit when he wanted to leave.

"This will have to do me boys."

"Yeah we gotta go too, look man," Muscat grabbed Sandy's forearm. "We can never repay you for saving us today, now what we told you tonight is true. I know you'll go looking for that boat one day and I hope you find it and when you do don't forget who told you. Look there are a lot of fellas out there who have an interest in this but, they don't know where it is. I'm prepared to cut you in. Forget the rest of them. You and me go 50/50."

"What is the special cargo?"

"You'll know it when you see it." The fat man could tell by the look on Sandy's face that he had him hooked.

"You've got a deal." And with that Sandy offered his hand on a gentleman's agreement.

Out the front of the restaurant while waiting for Sandy's cab the big Italian pulled a couple of business cards from his wallet and handed one to Sandy.

"Put your name on the back of that one so that we have your details." He then took the pen and wrote a series of numbers divided by a forward slash on the back of the other.

"What's that?"

"That my friend is the position of the boat radioed through on the mayday the night she went down."

CHAPTER 9

THE REPORTER

The reporter from the Examiner who had missed Sandy in the afternoon was still waiting in the cane lounge when the reluctant hero returned from dinner that night. "A minute if you would Mr. Horder." The rumpled looking fellow who kept irregular hours put down the crossword from his own paper to greet his subject.

Sandy picked the guy in one and straight away decided to nip the story in the bud. "Yes."

"Edward Pollock from the Port Stephens Examiner, I'd like to do the story of the rescue out there today," the newsman said indicating to the now dark bay and beyond.

"Yes," Sandy said for the second time, "it got a bit rough, but everything turned out for the best."

"The story at the Fishing Club evolved around you. I thought you might like to expand on some of the incidents that happened out there today."

"Sure, sure, the bar's closed but we can sit over here for a while," Sandy moved over to a comfortable corner fabric lounge.

The reporter pulled a hand sized pad and a flick top pen from his shirt pocket. "These two fellows in the small boat, I'd like to get their story, what happened to them?"

"I don't know."

"The feeling is that they were holiday makers, who got caught in a small boat in a rough sea."

"Sounds feasible," Sandy shrugged his shoulders.

"And you actually went in the water after one of them?"

"No, no," Sandy objected, "we threw in a lifebuoy and a rope and then dragged him on board."

"You got the motor going when everyone thought all was lost?"

"Ah jammed starter motor, get a spanner on the end of the shaft, you'd know about that wouldn't you?"

"No" The reporter looked down at his empty note pad and tried a new angle.

"I believe you live here at the Country Club Mr. Horder?"

"Yes."

"Holidaying?"

"Extended," the interviewee hesitated giving the impression some things were private.

"Where do you call home?"

"Hey, next thing you'll be asking me is my age," Sandy made light of the meeting to throw the fellow off.

Edward Pollock knew enough to pick a fellow who didn't want to be found. Anonymity was a curtain that men with women troubles or money troubles preferred to hide behind. "You know Mr. Horder; most people like to get their picture in the paper." The reporter said as he folded his note book and touched the button on the top of his ball point.

"I can understand that." Sandy replied.

"I'll respect your privacy," the reporter was genuine.

"The story will be written up as a misadventure. No names, no pack drills."

"Fine."

Because of his privileged life style Sandy, who was a permanent resident of the Country Club and seen now as a disinclined champion added another chapter to his story, that of respect.

His fishing companions who were used to shoulder shrugging had accepted his likening for privacy and in their silence showed him their respect. The townsfolk, who had fanned the tale on rumour, couldn't always find the hero to worship, when they did see him in the street they smiled and nodded, they looked for notice but wouldn't step over the privacy line, thus showing their respect.

After tea alone in the very busy dining room at the Country Club most nights, the establishment's acclaimed guest would retire to the balcony of his suite, sip a good whisky, gaze over the beautiful black image that was Shoal Bay, and wonder about Sandy Horder the person he had created. It was unintentional. He was looking for obscurity but found esteem.

As always the man would delve into the created personage of Sandy Horder. As always he convinced himself he was Sandy Horder. Emit Horsley was the odd one out.

Emit Horsley the cleaner from the Technical College who sat in the corner bar of the Bowling Club in suburban Perth on Saturday afternoon with his brother and an old school mate, almost went unnoticed. Emit Horsley was the yes man worker, the yes man husband who was destined to live and die in Bulwer Street, the street of the underdog.

Emit Horsley who abandoned his wife and daughter and absconded with a fortune not his own, was a person he did not want to know. He never thought 'what would they say if they could see me now.' No, Sandy Horder never gave Bulwer Street another thought, Shoal Bay was his home and his life now.

And then there were these two strangers who turned up on the high seas with a story that could be as big as his own secret. 'You'll know it when you see it,' Muscat's words became the thought Sandy went to bed with, the thought that woke him each morning.

If there was a treasure out there and he could claim it, this could legitimize his own dilemma. Sunken treasures tend to have an adventurous mysterious romance woven into them, and the value of the prize is always incalculable.

What is under the sea and what is under the back seat of the car becomes one.

CHAPTER 10

SANDY'S NEW BOAT

It was Sandy Horder who found The Tigress at Lake Macquarie a beautiful twenty eight foot cruiser all white and stainless steel. The timberwork in the galley and the forward section was light oak and matched the deck.

"There's twin Volvo V six marines under here," the salesman said as he lifted the timber hatch with a counter sunk stainless steel ring. "The owner was one of those 'thought he was invincible clever dick sort of blokes'" he expanded.

Sandy Horder stroked his chin and nodded. He knew the salesman would tell the whole story with out to much prompting.

"Yes bought this craft new, had it all refitted to his specifications, ripped the Mercuries out and plonked these two in. Wanted it to go." he hesitated. "And go she does."

Sandy looked into the engine bay, the four chromed rocker covers and polished aluminium flexi-pipes contrasted the red fiberglass enclosure. She looked hot.

"What? Found something better?" Sandy asked. This boat caught Sandy's eye from the street above the Marina. It was beautiful, he wanted to know its history, and then he would buy it.

"Na, the silly bastard went broke. The car boys took back the Jag and we got this little beauty. A thirty five year old swimming pool builder can you believe it?" the salesman lowered the hatch and twisted the stainless steel ring.

"You won't find a better boat than this in its class, overcapitalized to hell, that's what fellows like this do," the salesman went on philosophizing. "They think they're the only ones who know how to make money, they trail-blaze the boat industry the car blokes can't build big enough cars for them, the best house isn't good enough. They have no respect for money." He concluded, he wasn't looking for an argument and he didn't get one.

"Fine I'll buy it, I'll be paying cash."

The boat salesman almost swallowed his tongue then grasped for his composure.

"Ah, yes, you, I um move rather quickly."

"No respect for money." Sandy allowed a smile as he looked directly at the salesman.

"Look I don't um….." the Salesman was finding it hard to finish sentences.

"The name doesn't suit the craft," Sandy changed to a new tact.

"Yes Mr……. what was your name I'm sorry?"

"Horder, Sandy Horder."

"Horder, Sandy Horder." The salesman repeated exactly in his nervous stammer.

"Yes we will change the name and register it for you."

"Let's kick it over." Sandy lifted the engine bay hatch.

"Yes sir, Mr. Horder I'll get the keys," the salesman hadn't sold a boat all month, last month wasn't much better and he was showing his hand, he was at the buyer's mercy.

When the salesman returned a couple of minutes later carrying a battery starter Sandy was standing near the open engine bay hatch holding the 'For Sale' sign. "I'd like to hear these go."

The salesman looked at the sign in Sandy's hand. He had this one in the bag so kept on the positive note. "Oh you will, we'll take her out to the heads, you can have her once we are out of the Marina."

Sandy held the hatch as the still nervous salesman attached the starter.

"She hasn't been started for a while."

"Understand."

"Are you from around here?" The salesman felt better as he was doing something with his hands.

"No I'll be taking her up to the Bay."

"That's a nice run from here," he looked up, "you'll do it in an hour."

"It won't be me; I haven't got a boat licence."

The salesman looked up again as he tested the connections. "You're buying a boat like this – you haven't got a licence?"

"I'll get one."

"She's a big one to start on."

"That's what I like about her."

Sandy held the hatch cover as the salesman got up. "I'll kick her over," the excited salesman said as he climbed up the few steps to the wheel. The four rocker covers shook on the third kick, Sandy smiled. In five minutes they were away from the Marina and in the beautiful calm waters of the lake.

"I shouldn't do this but would you like to take her for a while?" The salesman and Sandy changed places, the latter needed no tuition, his left hand grabbed the wheel between the nine o'clock and twelve positions, his right gripped the joining bar on the two power levers protruding from the dashboard. He pulled the levers down slowly, watched the tachometer and turned slightly left. The big craft responded instantly to the power and turn.

Sandy nodded and pulled the wheel back past straight and then to the right at the same time applying more power as he had watched Steve do.

Now he smiled. He felt the instant power she was beautiful. The previous owner had spent his money well and it was a pity, Sandy thought that he couldn't have held on to it. Sandy straightened it again and pulled the levers back, the muffled drone lifted the bow.

"Whoa, whoa" the nervous salesman grabbed the stainless steel rail, "you like 'em to go."

"Yes she does that," Sandy pushed the levers back to normal speed, the torque was good, a bit like the Statesman, he was very pleased.

"Thanks for the drive," he looked at the boatman.

"Do you want me to take her back?"

"Yes, I'm satisfied."

Back at the Marina Sandy was introduced to Mr. Freeburn the owner of Saltwater Marine, and over a coffee he kept comparing him with another fellow he had met. Muscat the

Italian, who he had pulled out of the sea on that memorable day not so long ago. He realized the common thread was boats and the sea, but they were two different men.

The Italian was a real businessman who had tried everything and would probably keep it up until he died and then would leave no debt. In fact he offered half of whatever treasure that was lying on the ocean floor to Sandy for saving his life!

Mr. Freeburn on the other hand, to Sandy's summing up was all front, unpaid debt was his bonus.

"Look gentlemen if you could see your way clear to peel thirty thousand off that boat I'll bring the money down tomorrow."

"Mr. Horder we couldn't do that." The flashy boss man thought the deal was in the bag.

"That's my offer."

"We may be able to shave some for a quick sale," Freeburn didn't want to let this one go.

"Oh it'll be quick; the money will be here tomorrow less thirty grand." He finished his sentence and rubbed his index finger across his brow.

"That's my only offer." Sandy wouldn't normally do that. Emit Horsley would never do it. Why he paid top dollar for the Statesman without thinking of bargaining. But Emit wasn't here, and Sandy didn't like the flashy boss at all, not one little bit.

The boat was bought at a creditor's auction. There was a lot of money tied up in it and people were not buying boats at the moment.

CHAPTER 11

THE SUGAR BAY

Sandy Horder got the call from reception a half an hour earlier on returning from his morning walk. He showered, changed and was headed for the front door when the ever friendly receptionist smiled. "They said they would be waiting at the wharf for you Mr. Horder."

"Thank you."

It looked stunning sitting at high tide near the weighing gantry on the old wharf. The beautiful white sleek speedy lines enhanced with natural light oak trim and bold stainless steel railings, the name *Sugar Bay* done in red shadowed in grey branded her as Sandy's own.

It took Sandy three days to get his boating licence but rumours were out there the first day, the new boat on the bay was Sandy's.

"Well boys," Sandy, lifted his glass at the usual R.S.L. afternoon drinks "we're back in the fishing business, the *Sugar Bay* will leave the Country Club wharf at 7 in the morning."

Maurice couldn't get to his feet to respond, the smile on his face said it all. He spoke for the crew, "We'll all be there."

After the big sea rescue Maurice lost his confidence in skippering a boat and sold the *White Zephyr* but every morning he watched and identified each craft that went towards the heads from his veranda. This gave him the chance to do what he came to the Bay to do, to fish. With Sandy at the helm, he and his friends would go to the South Pole.

At seven the next morning, the crew were on board. This was a new era. Nobody thought of the dangers of the sea until that treacherous day when nature and mechanical mishap hit them with everything. Now nobody gave it a thought because Sandy was in charge. Now it's Sandy and the *Sugar Bay.*

"Give it a go here fellows?" he said as he backed off the power 40 minutes out of port. He turned on the large sophisticated monitor and checked his position both lateral and longitudinally. He allowed the two Volvos to idle the craft to the position he wanted.

Maurice was baited and ready as he looked to the Captain for approval.

Sandy sensed the anticipation, smiled at the old man and cut the motors.

"Ok let's fish."

Five lines went into a calm sea. Sandy looked at the screen and fine-tuned it with a half round dial at the side and watched an image form. In a minute he shook his head, he rubbed his index finger along his bottom lip mesmerized by the blue black glow. He looked away and blinked as you would at night before looking back to get the fresh look.

"Those screens can do that to you," said Steve.

"Yes" a forefinger and thumb spread across Sandy's forehead. He looked again, and he blinked. He said the longitudinal and lateral softly to himself as he ran his fingers along the edges of the monitor.

"Must be a big fish," laughed Steve.

"Yes she's a beauty!" Sandy could not believe his luck in such a big ocean. First shot.

Sandy checked his position top and side, he had memorized the numbers on the business card the Italian had given him, and they were the same. There was a big object straight below. "Well that was easy" he said softly again.

"What do you see?" Steve was drawn to electronic instruments as much as he was to fishing itself. To him it was all part of the fish catching game.

"Fish and more fish, they can't hide down there," Sandy took the general approach.

The Skipper looked to the horizon, then back to the screen. He checked the depth memorized it then stared at the dark image. It could be the shape of a large boat sitting in an upright position as if it had gone straight down. But Sandy's imagination could be at play.

"We have a winner," Jimmy yanked his rod let it slacken then pulled the dancing fish across the placid water.

"You haven't got it in the boat yet!" Dick said as he watched the fish do all its tricks to escape the inevitable. The little Pole was good at the next part. Work the reel, lift the rod and swing the prize into his left hand.

"Bad luck Dickie, ya just lost ten bucks," Jimmy was referring to the ten dollars each man contributed to the running of the boat for the mornings fishing and the reward for the first catch was no fee. Dick never won and he didn't like it.

Sandy turned off the screen and baited up, he didn't want the boys to know yet why he was really out here. The next step would be to look more closely.

His mind wasn't on the fishing; his thoughts were 'how can I pull this off? A diver, that's what I need.' Hmm…

CHAPTER 12

THE DIVER

"You want to get a bit closer to them?" Rod the shop assistant in the bait and tackle shop approached Sandy as he examined the scuba equipment.

"Yes," Sandy was fishing, this time for information. "I've always been interested in exploring the depths," he lied, "is it difficult to handle this gear?"

"Have you ever done any skin diving?"

"No."

"I run a couple of classes at Fingal Bay from novice to advanced weekday afternoons if that could be of any help?"

Sandy looked thoughtfully at the gear and wondered.

"Is there something that you want to see or do you just want to look under the water?" the salesman asked.

"There's a wreck out there that I'm interested in." Sandy said.

"Oh there's quite a few," Rod smiled. "which one?"

"I don't know the name….."

"Oh pity," Rod said as he walked over to a colourful map on the side wall. "This is a copy of our immediate coastline," he touched the edges to the right and left, "these dark green spots, and there are several, are the wrecks that have been identified. There are others we know of but haven't found yet.

They say," he went on, "satellite scanning and photography will reveal all one day."

"Very interesting," Sandy looked closely at the map he picked up the coordinates he had memorized on the top and followed them down to the lateral line without being too obvious. There was no dark green spot.

"We have dived on most of these wrecks," Rod explained looking at Sandy. "As a matter of fact a friend of yours, the ex-pilot fellow is a very keen diver."

"Steve Flint?"

"Yes Steve did his training in the Air Force a very capable under water man."

"Really?"

That afternoon at the RSL Sandy walked into the gaming room as he did two or three times a week, put a hundred dollar note into two machines and played the maximum lines. Sometimes he won, when he did it was big but if he didn't win he had still laundered two hundred dollar notes.

"No jackpots today Sandy."

"I'll keep trying," Sandy answered the cashier as he walked out into the lounge area with one hundred and eighty dollars in broken down notes in his pocket. No one would question the rich hero from the west who liked to punt, dine out and drink and who was now the owner of one of the finest boats moored in Shoal Bay.

"Schooner Sandy?"

"Thanks Flash"

There was no one in the lounge at all.

"I'm first here," Sandy looked around as he pulled a ten dollar note from his pocket. "Take one out for yourself" he said to the barman. Flash loved black beer and even though drinking on duty was a sackable offence the best beer of the day was the sneaky one he had with the town hero, a simple gesture but appreciated because of who he was.

"Thank you Sandy," the barman said as he filled two glasses.

Everyday Sandy Horder spent some time on the boat. He would clean the cabin and the decks, go around the hull with along handle broom then rinse everything with fresh water. He couldn't leave those motors alone, he would just kick them over, and then it would be just a quick burst to the heads and back. Then it was out to the treasure and back. It became the 'Treasure' because the Italian said it was. It was exactly where he said it would be. He wondered what it was.

CHAPTER 13

GOLD COAST

Paradise Marine was the place to go if you were shopping for a boat on the Gold Coast. They catered for the rich. The people who bought the very best kept them at the high end marinas for entertaining purposes and eventually traded them in on something bigger and better.

Paradise Marine had just what they were looking for. They combed the opulent markets of Asia to bring back the best overpowered over optioned exclusive craft for the hungry gregarious types.

Johnnie Paradise was the man to know. Everyone in the know knew the gaudy Italian in colourful shirts and loud ties. Yes everyone knew Johnnie, the Tax Department were regular visitors as were Department of Fair Trading. The State Department of Marine Services and the local constabulary occasionally paid social visits. This is what makes a colourful identity, it keeps people talking and it's good for business.

One such person who was keeping an eye on the Paradise Marine was Derrick Fullerton a petty crook who was known to the police. He was on a watch list, and was occasionally questioned on matters relating to break ins. He was held some years ago on a drug distribution case where one party was callously bashed but refused to give evidence. Derrick Fullerton was subsequently let go. From then on he distanced himself from that business and concentrated on the lucrative break and enters profession on the unsuspecting holiday makers who swarmed Australia's favourite holiday destination every year.

Derrick worked the cleaner's hours, dark till dawn. Money changed hands as did keys.

The routine was, couples would go out for dinner and Derrick would go through their rooms. Now this thief believed in ongoing business. He didn't want the cops or an investigation closing down his little enterprise, so it was a set of earrings here, a few dollars out of a wallet there multiplied by six or eight rooms a night four nights a week. Nice takings.

Derrick Fullerton was squaring up with his fence one afternoon in the back room of a pawn shop when he first heard the name Ivan Sandvic.

"I'd never heard of him either," the fence was telling Derrick. "He's the biggest thing in Eastern Europe, manufactured stuff. He's got a pill for everything."

"So what? Is he going to elbow his way onto the coast?"

"Don't think so, they say he's an eccentric, collects art and artifacts, he goes to any lengths. Half the stolen masterpieces of the world end up in Ivan Sandvic's collection."

"So is there a valuable art collection on the Gold Coast?"

'No but a priceless collection passed through the Coast some years ago."

"And?" Derrick Fullerton was hooked.

"The story I heard was that it was some of the valuables pilfered during the Second World War that ended up in Asia then eventually smuggled out of Hong Kong after they went independent."

"You lost me. What's this got to do with anything?" Derrick came back to the job at hand and held up a pearl necklace.

The fence hadn't finished. He played his last card.

"Johnnie Paradise buys his big cruisers up in Asia; the story is it all came through his place."

"Johnnie Paradise he is a slippery one."

"The big cruisers used to fill up there in the middle of the night and head south before dawn."

"How long ago was this?" Derrick was suddenly getting interested.

"Years ago."

"Why the interest now?"

"The particular cruiser with the real cache on board never made it to its destination. They tell me the connection down south reckons someone knows where it is. It sounds to me like Johnnie Paradise. Now Ivan Sandvic has put out a contract for information for four hundred thousand dollars."

If Ivan the terrible is as big as you say. I wouldn't want to be Johnnie Paradise."

"He's gone missing."

CHAPTER 14

IVAN SANDVIC

Ivan Sandvic sank in an overly comfortable leather lounge crossed his legs and found the right place for his elbows in the soft cushioned arm rests.

"What's the latest?" the burly Russian intimidated Derrick Fullerton sitting opposite on an equally plush lounge in a private Learjet sitting on the tarmac at Brisbane Airport. Before he could answer, Ivan Sandvic raised his right arm snapped his finger and pointed to an attendant standing at the entrance to the stateroom. He beckoned him with his index finger. Out of nowhere a finely rolled Cuban cigar appeared on a silver tray. It was unwrapped put back on the silver tray and handed to Ivan who rolled the distinctive power symbol between his thumb and forefinger, then looked up to the servant for a light.

"Well?"

"There is an outfit in Southport called Paradise Marine they are Asian importers and I believe that they have had a lot to do with mysterious shipping movements out of Asia over the years."

Derrick had no contact with Paradise Marine he was merely trying to get the four hundred thousand dollar contract for information leading to the recovery of ancient artifacts.

The big Russian didn't take his eyes off his Derrick. He took small frequent draws from his cigar and worked him out to be just the small time crook that he was.

"I give you four hundred thousand dollars now, you deliver in four months"

What? This small time crook had just hit the big time. He could hardly contain himself.

"Pick up the money on the way out." Ivan ordered. "We meet 13th of August you will have the information I need."

Money up front, unbelievable Derrick Fullerton thought, why didn't the fence take this job himself instead of giving it to me?

If Derrick Fullerton had any idea of who he was dealing with, he would have left the money, the lear jet and Surfers Paradise and never looked back. Ivan Sandvic was not a man you should disappoint.

CHAPTER 15

THE HUNT BEGINS

Derrick Fullerton had been watching Paradise Marine for some time and had discovered that the little Italian outfit was, in the main, a maintenance facility to the local fishing industry. The Italians were brought to this crook's attention after Ivan Sandvic put out the contract to find the eighty foot cruiser that had escaped his boys enroute to the Australian east coast.

The coincidence was the very expensive high powered craft that started turning up at Paradise Marine, staying overnight, refuelling, and then moving on to places unknown. The eighty footer wasn't seen as yet, but the four hundred thousand dollar contract was much too alluring for Derrick Fullerton to let slip by. He was contracted by Ivan Sandvic to deliver the lost eighty footer in four months for $400,000-00. As usual the money was up front and your time starts now.

Derrick Fullerton was also a big and frightening man in his domain. As with all people in his profession he ruled with force, but the thought of what might happen was usually enough for a foe to see things his way. He had a plan to extract the information he needed from the Italians and he was about to put it into action.

The hearsay about the lost eighty footer was quietly rumbling around the waterfront. The word was Muscat

Farincini and his big mate Dominic had a flying trip down the coast somewhere on a hot lead.

Derrick Fullerton watched the two every afternoon. They would leave work together in an old High Ace van, drive two blocks to Liquorland, pick up two bottles of red wine and go back to Muscat's place. After an hour or so Dominic would appear, the little worse for wear, jump into the High Ace and drive the two blocks to his own home.

Muscat was the smart one, Dominic the dope.

The day before operation talkfest Derrick Fullerton went through the plan with his accomplice. "You've got the car."

"Yep, got it last night, it's in my garage."

"Now, we need plenty of stuff."

"Oh yeah, we got plenty of stuff, I'm going to like this job."

"Good, the stuff has got to be under the car, it's got to look spectacular."

"Oh she's going to go up."

"Good, now because that building site has shut down we can have all that side of the street. The foot path is shut so there are no pedestrians, so park the car in front of the building site boarding and wait for my signal."

"I can't wait. This bloke is going to shit himself."

The next day right on cue Dominic waltzed out of the bottle shop not a care in the world.

"Hey"

"Who me?"

"That's right."

Derrick Fullerton grabbed the Italian by the arm. Poor Dominic secured his two bottles; he wasn't going to let them go.

"See the green car over there," Derrick paused and increased his grip.

"Yes! Yes! I see, I see."

"In one minute it's going to blow to bits."

Dominic looked at his assailant then at the green car, he was in the grip of terror.

"I want you to tell me who you saw down the coast in relation to the treasure," Derrick hesitated. "The big boat. Who's got the big boat?"

"I know nothing," it could have been a line out of a T.V. show.

"In a half a minute the green car goes up, and there's a bomb on the front step of your house."

Derrick pulled out a mobile phone with his free hand. "I press eight, it goes off."

Things went bad for poor Dominic, the front of his work shorts instantly was soaked, and it ran down his leg over his boot protectors onto the footpath.

"Who's your contact?" the big crook put more pressure on the Italian's arm at the same time nodding to his accomplice Bruno the bomber, down on the next corner.

Everything seemed to happen in slow motion. Time stopped, the loudest explosion in history built up to a crescendo. The green car went fifteen feet into the air then smashed and blew up on top of the derelict building. Poor Dominic's bowels let go, and ran down the other leg onto the footpath the stench was unbearable. In real time this was a second.

"Sandy Horder! Sandy Horder!"

"Where do I find him?"

"Shoal Bay! Shoal Bay!"

People ran, some to the explosion, some away from it. Fear and disbelief gripped everyone in the immediate area. Dominic was hysterical. He hobbled as best he could in his distasteful state toward the van still clutching the two bottles of red wine.

Muscat was huddled into the passenger seat, his head in the crash position between his legs. "What happen?" the muffled strained voice of Muscat came from the near the floor.

"The man he kill me, he kill my family, he blowup car, he blow up Sandy Horder." Dominic was yelling and jabbering like a maniac.

"What!" Muscat sat upright.

"What is that smell?" he looked at Dominic. "What happened to you, get out."

Poor Dominic in his dirty shorts was verging on a complete mental breakdown. He twisted the key on the steering column, dropped the two bottles of wine on the middle seat, pushed the accelerator and clutch to the floor shoved the column gear lever into first and dropped the clutch.

The van jumped forward just clipping the car in front of him as he fought with the wheel.

"Look out," Muscat pointed and shouted at people running everywhere on the road as they now scrambled for their lives out of the path of the lunatic in the van.

"What happened?" Muscat looked at Dominic as he pushed the gears through, his eyes wide and bulging, his hair wet with perspiration all he had on his mind was how he must get away.

"Stop!" A lady stepped off the curb; the brake pedal almost went to the floor. The two wine bottles flew forward onto the dash and then smashed on the floor. This momentarily distracted Dominic who was committed to taking the next turn left, that split second had the van across the centre line where he side swiped a car coming in the opposite direction.

Muscat said nothing he prepared himself to meet his maker. As the van was gathering speed again, he joined his hands looked out through the front windscreen to the heavens and said something very solemnly in Italian.

This didn't work Dominic went screaming through a red light in second gear. The driver of car on his right did everything possible to stop. He stood on the brake pedal and swerved to the left there was a loud bang as he hit the rear of the van and spun it across the intersection.

Muscat lashed out at Dominic with his closed right fist, the back of which caught the driver on the left cheek. The madman again ground the gear-lever into first and at full revs dropped the clutch thrusting the van again through the traffic in a vain bid to get away from the evil place that set him off less than a minute ago.

This man who had literally done it in his pants run amuck through the streets and left the scene of two accidents in that last minute was now the most wanted man in the state.

Muscat had had enough, his used to be friend, was now driving up a residential street in first gear as hard as the engine would push it. He undid his seat belt and grabbed the wheel, two things you should never do. The van went up and over the gutter and through a front fence.

That was three accidents. "Get out!" The frightened driver now in shock glared at Muscat who had leaned over opened the driver's door and pushed him out.

"Get in the back you stink like a…."

Dominic got to his feet and scrambled to the back door. Muscat slid across and into a filthy sticky seat just as a lady came to the front door of the house with the now busted front fence. Muscat was a worse driver than his 'used to be friend' Dominic. He found every gear but reverse and knocked the previous driver over twice in the process of extracting the van from the front fence.

The lady stood in disbelief as she watched this clip from a Charlie Chaplin movie being played out in her front garden. Eventually the van sped off down the normally quiet street the back door open with poor Dominic half hanging out screaming for forgiveness.

Muscat unfamiliar with the old van and off the accustomed track home, made blunders in road rules and homeward direction, this with the odour of cheap red wine and the foul mess left by his 'used to be friend' had him cursing in his native tongue and thumping the steering wheel.

"Please get me to my family," Dominic begged as he hung onto the wire mesh grill that separated the load area of the van from the cabin. Muscat slammed on the brakes; Dominic used the rule of physics to plant his face firmly into the grill that he had been hanging onto with both hands.

"I'll get you home alright as soon as I find my way out of wherever I am," the driver raged in anger not understanding anything that happened in the last two and a half minutes.

"The man," Dominic started, now kneeling on the floor of the loading area in the back and using his hands as only Italians do.

"Shudup about the man," Muscat was now over the edge, reality went out the door when his 'used to be friend', went through the fence. He pushed the leaver into first without the clutch, the grinding meshing sound of cogs on cogs tail shaft clunking on gearbox and the four cylinder peak revving wasn't quite enough notice for poor Dominic who frantically grabbed for the wire mesh grill that separated load area from cabin. That rule of physics now worked in reverse as the passenger rolled head over turkey out the opened back door.

The police arrived at the now terrorist like explosion scene at the same time Muscat was lifting his now best friend, who he had almost killed, into the back of the most sought after van in the country.

"You say it was a Mitsubishi?" Sergeant Green asked a willing witness.

"Yes a Mitsubishi."

"What colour was it?"

"It was sort of grey."

"Not white?" they were almost always white the copper thought.

"No sort of grey."

"Any signwriting, logos, that sort of thing?"

"Don't think so."

"Come on sir, you would remember a sign on a speeding van, this is very important it is the first terrorist attack on the Gold Coast."

"Sir I thought I was going to die, you should have heard the explosion. What do you think gets a car up there?" the unreliable eye witness pointed to the burning car.

Don't upset the witness, the police rule, try another tact.

"Did you notice anything else?"

"Yeah." The witness screwed up his face.

"The guy ran funny," he mimicked the style.

"Throwing his weight from one leg to the other, like keeping his legs apart."

The Channel Ten crew had a line of people wanting to get on television.

"You say they got away in a Toyota Hi Ace?"

"Yeah tore down there," the bystander pointed, "clipped a car going 'round the corner!"

"Did you notice anything unusual?"

"Yeah the terrorist bloke ran funny."

A couple of hours later Dominic turned up at Muscat's front door.

"Come in, come in, you're alright?" he asked.

"Yes," Dominic was embarrassed.

"Ah you're all cleaned up?"

Dominic didn't want to talk about that, he looked away.

"It's alright, the family is out, we talk."

The two men walked into a comfortable lounge room where a bottle of red stood opened on the coffee table; a big screen television was running continuous news of the terrorist attack on the Gold Coast.

"Here, sit down, we drink."

"They think it's a terrorist attack, they are looking for us," Muscat opened proceedings.

"It was terror." Dominic's eyes widened again, as he looked at the scene on the television.

"No," Muscat almost laughed, "they think it was terrorist you know a bomb.

"It was a bomb." Dominic looked in horror at the devastation.

"O.K. O.K. What did happen?"

"This man," Dominic started, still mesmerized by the television, "he grab," he stood up. "That man" Dominic put his glass down and pointed to the right hand side of the screen. "That man, he grab me, he say I blow up car, I blow your family, I blow up Sandy Horder."

"How does he know about Sandy Horder?"

"I tell him."

"Why?"

"He say he blow up my family."

"O.K. stop." Muscat puts things in their right perspective.

"The man grabs you."

"Yes, he say I blow up car."

"Why?

"He pull out phone," Dominic takes his own phone from his trousers pocket.

"He say, I press eight I blow up your house."

Muscat looked at his once again best friend put his arm out to console him.

"The car she blows up I shit myself."

"Yeah, yeah, don't worry about that. Did you fix the van?"

"I hose it out."

"Keep it in your shed the cops are looking for it."

"They should look for the man." The news tape kept running, the same scenes were repeated.

"There he is again."

"Tell me about Sandy Horder." Muscat didn't expect anyone to be onto them.

"The man say, who's got the big boat?"

Muscat nodded.

"He hold his phone, he say who did you see down the coast?"

"I say Sandy Horder, he was going to blow up my family."

"It's O.K." Muscat nodded again.

"We are going to Shoal Bay."

Shoal Bay was beautiful. It was mid-April the waters were like glass, the cloudless sky mimicked the water. Dominic stopped the rental over the road from the Country Club with a good view of the wharf. A glistening white cruiser was tied up.

"I wonder if that's him," Muscat said, "let's go and have a look."

The two Italians looked out of place as they strode out along the wharf, Muscat in his dark trousers, unmatched coat and navy tee shirt and Dominic in his baggy jeans black shirt and sandals. Sandy picked them as a couple of tourists looking for a conversation until they came into recognition range.

"Well fancy seeing you again," the ship's Captain put down his cleaning gear. "Come aboard."

They all shook hands heartily.

"This yours?" Muscat asked.

"Yes," Sandy smiled as he cast a proud eye around the boat, "bought her a couple of months ago."

"Very nice vessel." Muscat looked and patted the railing.

"Have you found the wreck yet?"

Wrecks and treasures are not the everyday talking point, but somehow Sandy knew that these two men would be back when he found it.

"Yes I have."

"Really, already?" Muscat was amazed.

"Your reference numbers led me straight to it."

"Anything else?" The Italian knew the right man was on the job.

"No," Sandy Horder smiled and shook his head, "I know where she is but I haven't gone any further than that."

"You're amazing you know that," Muscat reached out and took the skipper's hand.

"And this boat," the Italian looked around admiringly "it's, it's what I expected you to have."

"Yes this boat made the job easy, she's got the depth gauges and screens and I knew I was on the money it was right on the two reference lines."

"What are you going to do?" The Italian was glad his lifesaver had found the wreck. He needed to warn his friend on the impeding danger that he was now in. "They got your name."

Muscat told the day old story.

"That has been on the news, it was a terrorist attack."

"No, she no terrorist attack this a big deal, I don't know who behind it, that attack was all about the boat."

"Poor Dominic here," Muscat shook his friend's shoulder, "he was the, how you say, scapegoat. I sorry Sandy Horder."

"Hey it's alright."

"The explosion was just to show him they mean business, they threatened his family."

"Whose they?"

"We dunno." Two arms out- stretched, hands turned up.

"They got your name my friend."

Sandy stroked his chin. He pushed his already conceived plans forward.

"What about you fellows, what are you going to do?"

"We help however we can," Muscat spoke for the Italians.

"Where are you staying?"

"Nowhere."

"We'll get you a place back up in Nelson Bay, lay low for a couple of days." Sandy was enjoying this.

"Hey," Muscat objected, "they know us, that's how they know about you."

"That's why we have got to move," I'll take this back to the mooring, go to the front bar of the Country Club," he pointed to the watering hole. "I'll meet you there in twenty minutes."

Exactly twenty minutes later Sandy Horder walked in through the side door of the front bar.

"You're a bit early Sandy," the barman said. "Your little mate's over there, are you going to have one?"

"Thanks George and one for Jimmy." Sandy put twenty on the bar and looked around for the Italians, they weren't there.

He carried the two beers over to Jimmy Zininski.

"Try this on,"

"Oh you shouldn't have," a bit of bar room banter.

"The Italians are back."

"What?"

"The two Italians we met on the high seas a couple of months ago," Sandy looked around the few early drinkers, "they're back in town."

"What for?" Jimmy Zininski drank from his glass.

It was strange, Sandy Horder knew about the treasure, he had bought a powerful boat to look for it, found it, discussed it with the Italians, but had shared none of this with his friends. He walked over to the bar.

"George did two Italian fellows come in here before me this morning?"

"No, I've been on since opening Sandy." He walked back to the window table he and Jimmy shared.

"That's funny," he shook his head.

"What's up?"

"The Italians, I was to meet them here."

"When did you see them?"

"About twenty minutes ago," Sandy looked out on the bay thoughtfully, "I was out on the wharf playing around with the boat, I took it back to the mooring and said I'd meet them here."

"May be they went next door." There was a coffee lounge in the adjoining the bar.

Sandy put his glass down, walked out the door down the footpath and into the coffee lounge. "Good morning Mr. Horder."

"Morning Pat," Sandy looked around the empty venue "Did you see two Italian men around here in the last ten minutes?"

"No," the waitress hesitated, "there was a bit of a scuffle out the front a while back, they were two Italian looking fellows, a man seemed to bundle them into a car."

"Yes he pushed one of them into the back seat. I don't think they wanted to go."

"Where did they go?"

"Towards Nelson Bay."

"You don't know what sort of car it was?" Sandy said as he walked to the door.

"It was red."

"How many of those have you had?" Sandy asked his little mate when he came back into the bar.

"This is me second, when I go and see George next, it'll be me turn," he gulped from his glass, "that'll be me third."

"Would you mind doing me a favour?" Sandy emptied his own glass.

"Yeah," the little fellow could see something was wrong.

"What are we doing?" Jimmy asked as he hurried after Sandy out of the bar.

"Where's your car?"

"'Round the corner, where're we going?"

"Nelson Bay, we are looking for a red car."

"That'll be easy," Jimmy teased as he got into the unlocked car.

Sandy got in and fastened his safety belt. "Let's try the Motels."

After driving from one to another they finally arrived at the Motel where Jimmy did the cleaning.

"There's a red car," Jimmy said excitedly, "It's a rental."

"How can you tell?"

"It's got a Qantas sticker on the back window."

"That'd be them, the guy would have flown down from Queensland," Sandy chewed on his thumbnail thoughtfully.

"What guy?"

"Wait a minute," Sandy thought, "you know them here, how about you go into and pick up a brochure or something, get a look at the bloke checking in, don't be obvious."

"Why? What's going on?

"I'll tell you later."

Jimmy got out of the car and casually strode across the gravel drive to the reception office. "Morning Marg.'

"Hello Jimmy what are you doing back so soon?"

"I got an old mate out in the car he needs a room tonight. I told him you've got the best place in town, but he's a bit mean he wants to look at the tariff can I take one of these?"

He reached across in front of the stranger signing in. "Excuse me sir," had a good look at him and noted the name.

"Tell your friend it's a serve yourself all you can eat breakfast."

"I'll sell it to him Marg."

Jimmy looked at the two Italians in the red car on his way past and he nodded at them. They obviously didn't recognize him.

"Did you get a look at him?" Sandy asked as Jimmy got back into his car.

"Yep"

"Will you know him again?"

"Yep and his name is Derrick Fullerton."

"Good Man."

"Now what's this all about?" The little fellow was now enjoying this.

Derrick Fullerton knew the Italians would lead him to the treasure through their man, the man he knew by name as Sandy Horder. He simply flew to Williamtown Airport and was on the lookout at every plane that came in from Queensland until they arrived. He saw them rent a car and then followed the unsuspecting pair to Shoal Bay. He watched through his binoculars as they walked along the wharf to be greeted by a Skipper of a larger cruise. This had to be his man.

Derrick Fullerton seemed to be holding all the cards, what he didn't know was that the man he had in his sights was now watching him. One problem Derrick had was what to do with his captives, he had confiscated their phones, and had

Dominic wetting himself every time he pulled out his own phone and mentioned the number eight.

He pulled out said phone looked at Dominic then pressed some numbers.

"What are you doing?" Derrick said into the phone still staring at Dominic.

"Just waitin' for your orders boss." Bruno, the bomber said from the other end.

"O.K. your job is to get down here now," Derrick went on "drive down tonight, bring the gear," he explained, "guns, explosives, trick detonators, timers, ropes and of course the waterproof stuff."

"You said tonight?"

"Yes" Derrick looked at his watch. "I'll expect you at breakfast ring me when you get here," he hung up.

The Italians sat on a bed in the main bedroom, they were scared.

"You blokes hungry?"

"Yes," the friends answered together.

"No trouble." Derrick said. "Remember, eight," he pulled out his phone.

Dominic did all he could to stop the flow of the fluids, now the talk of guns and explosives, he was terrified.

"We'll get take away."

Derrick Fullerton drove around unfamiliar streets followed by Sandy and Jimmy a respectably distance back.

"Just like the movies," the boy in Jimmy was always there ready to come to the top.

"Where are they going?" this was the second time the two detectives followed the suspects down Magnus Street.

"May be they're trying to shake us," Jimmy carried on his foolishness.

The indicator went to the right this time around.

"I think they're lost," Sandy summed things up.

"Wrong," the indicator went left at the red and yellow sign.

"They are having McDonalds for lunch," Jimmy looked at his watch, "afternoon tea?"

The surveillance team parked in the street and watched the red car go around the drive through. The line of cars shuffled along stopping at the ordering station. "Can I take your order please?"

"What!"

"Can I take your order please?"

Derrick Fullerton looked angrily at the loudspeaker at his window.

"Can I take your order please?" He pressed the unfamiliar button on his car window.

"Yes, yes give us three hamburgers with the lot."

"Can I take your order please?"

"No make that six and chips I'm hungry."

"Can I take you order please?"

A car horn sounded from behind. Derrick went for the door handle. "I'll bury you, you."

"You gotta press the button," Dominic sobbed uncontrollably and wet himself yet again.

"Wonder what's keeping them," Jimmy asked when the cars stopped coming out of the drive through.

Derrick Fullerton was out of the car and pressing the button very hard.

"Listen sister get me six hamburgers, call 'em what you bloody well like and enough chips for three men." Then he walked back to the car behind. "O.K. dickhead you press that horn once more and you will meet your Grandfather again in heaven or hell. Now if it's hell I'll be looking out for you when I get there and I'll give you the floggin' of your life."

When the red car stopped at the service counter there were six hamburgers and six large chips presented with "Have a nice day."

CHAPTER 16

KIDNAPPED

The big four were at the Club and had been briefed by Jimmy Zininski before Sandy arrived that afternoon. Dick Walker pulled out the empty chair next to him for Sandy while Jimmy got the beers.

"Jimmy tells us the Italian fellows are back." It was Maurice Campbell who leaned across the table with the first question. "Are they in some kind of trouble?"

"I knew they were trouble when we pulled them out of the sea that day." Dick had Sandy's ear and hesitantly looked around the table for support. Dick was on his own here while the other three looked to Sandy. Sandy knew that Jimmy would tell the boys of their exploits today and this would wet their appetite for more.

"Yes they came out to the boat to see me this morning, to warn me." Sandy said just as Jimmy placed the tray of beers on the table.

"Warn you!" Dick turned in his chair to look Sandy in the eye. Five sets of eyes fixed themselves on him as well. The brief silence was broken by the town elder.

"What's going on son?" Maurice asked.

"There's sunken treasure out there." Sandy pointed through the panoramic window to the clam waters ahead.

"You had us there for a bit, Sandy." Jimmy said as he leaned back in his chair.

Steve Flint kept staring at Sandy, as did the old fellow Maurice. Dick and his mate Walt sniggered with Jimmy. Silence slowly fell like a veil over the table, the term 'warn me' seemed to be significant with sunken treasure.

"In a nutshell," Sandy started off to his now captive audience, "there is sunken treasure out there. I heard the story the night we rescued our Italian friends," he used the word 'we' when in fact it was he who brought both crews home safely. "They shouted me dinner and in appreciation for our efforts that day, they also gave me the grid bearings for a large cruiser that went down off the coast," he pointed, "out there."

"You bought the *Sugar Bay* with all the sonar gear and depth gauges" Steve pointed out, and then went on, "that first day we went out," his eyes narrowed, "you stopped a couple of miles out and checked the gear?"

"Yes."

"Did you find anything?"

"Yes."

"What? The sunken treasure?" said Walt in true sceptic tones.

"There's a cruiser down there," Sandy looked straight at Walt. They were all in disbelief.

"You have seen the actual boat?" Dick desperately wanted Just a yes or no answer.

"Well you don't see absolute objects Dick, but the gear on board picks up images. They can be magnified up to twenty times. There's a cruiser down there alright."

"Can you find it again?" Walt had reluctantly become a believer.

"I've been out there twenty times by myself. I knew where it was before the Italians came to warn me."

"What now?" Maurice asked.

Sandy Horder leaned forward in his chair, put his elbows on the table rested his chin on his clasped hands and spoke in a low tone. "Would you fellows be interested in bringing up this sunken treasure?" he paused. "It is achievable."

"Too right!" Walt jumped in, he had no idea how it would be done but he was definitely in.

"What about the Italians?" Maurice enquired as he leaned forward over the table.

"Jimmy here has been telling us how you two tracked them down and that they are being held captive."

"That's right," Sandy confirmed. "We've got to get them out."

"Can't you go to the police?" The old man asked.

"No."

"What then?"

"I think we should watch them, we have the advantage, they don't know us."

"They know you, and that's why they're here." Maurice said making a solid point.

"No," Sandy objected, "they know the cruiser went down here, and they know of Sandy Horder and probably the *Sugar*

Bay but they have never seen me or any of you." He thought
for a second. "May be they saw me from a distance when the
Italians came out to the wharf this morning, any way I could
wear a hat and dark glasses."

"And a moustache," Jimmy curled an index finger under his
nose. "Holmes."

Steve Flint looked at Jimmy, the finger quickly came down
and his smile froze.

"So we watch them, if they manage to get the information
out of the Italians and then it will be a race for the treasure."
was how Steve Flint saw it.

"The Italians might not talk."

Maurice and Steve seemed to be working out a plan.

"They'll talk." Steve was certain.

"So we watch them and see what happens." The old man
leaned back.

"Right," Sandy put his arms on the table in a plan making
gesture.

"If it's alright with everyone," Sandy lifted his hands,
"Jimmy and I will set ourselves up in his car out the front of
the Motel at seven in the morning. If another pair of you can
relieve us about ten in another car, then swap again at twelve
we won't be obvious. I'm sure we will know what's going
on by tomorrow afternoon." He hesitated and looked at each
man slowly. "Let's keep this to ourselves."

The next morning Jimmy pulled his car up opposite the
Motel, he could see the sunny courtyard, with the reception
area at the front, thus giving privacy to all the units. "I'll
take a look," Sandy got out of the car and strolled aimlessly

toward the reception gap. He noticed a Ford Falcon with interstate plates alongside the red car they'd been following the previous day. The boot lid was up as if someone was moving baggage into the only unit with the open door.

Inside he knew it was Dominic he saw because he was still wearing the same black clothes he wore yesterday. Two men came out of the unit and went to the car with the open boot. Derrick was doing all the talking and hurried Brunno along. They lifted two heavy looking bags from the car, had a quick look around and then he spotted Sandy. He immediately pushed Bruno toward the unit door.

He saw me Sandy thought but carried on like a wayward tourist.

"I think I blew it," Sandy said as he got back into the car. "I saw two fellows carrying something heavy into the Motel unit, and they saw me."

"How do you know that was our man?" Jimmy started to make some sense of it.

"The door was open and Dominic was inside."

"Oh, Dominic."

Sandy looked at his younger friend. He hadn't briefed the team well at all. He suddenly thought. They knew nothing about the bomb threat on Dominic's family. They didn't know about the treasure until yesterday, whereas Sandy himself had been planning to recover the treasure ever since the night Muscat told him about it. "Dominic is one of the Italians the other one is Muscat."

"You know them well?"

"Well enough for them to tell me about the treasure."

"What is the treasure?" Jimmy asked the question that had been overlooked.

"I was told I'll know it when I see it," Sandy answered.

Just then the red car came out of the Motel and drove straight past the two men.

"There they go," Jimmy started his car, "there was another bloke in the car."

"Gee I'd like to get a good look in that unit," Sandy said.

"They'll get away," Jimmy pointed through the windscreen.

"They won't leave the Bay," Sandy replied calmly, "can we get in that room?"

"No."

"You work here," Sandy pointed out.

"Reception faces every front door, the cleaners don't come in 'till after ten if that is of any help."

"Is there a back way in?"

"The bedrooms are at the front the bath rooms are at the back," Jimmy hesitated for a moment, "there is a back lane."

"Let's go, do you know which one it is from the back?"

"I'll just drive by, which one is it?"

"The blue Falcon is out the front."

"Right," the little cleaner said "four back from the top side."

The two men drove up the street, took the next right, then into a narrow lane way. A tall paling privacy fence would deter any would be intruder.

"Don't let the fence put you off; the ends are only dividing fences between the Motel and the neighbours, it's only four foot chain wire."

"Let's go."

They carefully and quietly climbed over the end fence and were now on forbidden turf. "Count them down one, two, three, four here we are." Jimmy looked at the small window.

"They always lock the front door, and they always leave the bathroom window open, to let the steam out."

"Good," Sandy wasn't here for a lesson he was already up on the sill. "This won't take long, keep an eye out."

Jimmy heard Sandy's leg go through the toilet seat, and then a hell of a noise in the early morning as the whole toilet suite smashed on the tile floor.

"You right?"

"Yes."

It was two minutes before another sound was heard.

"Get ready to take these." There was another crashing noise and water gushing under pressure as the cistern came off the wall under Sandy's weight.

"Did you get it?"

"What?"

A large sports bag appeared at the window.

"Yeah got it, what's that noise?"

"There's another one," Sandy ignored Jimmy's question.

"Yeah OK."

Then Sandy came out of the high window head first. He scrambled and twisted and landed right way up. "Oh that's a mess in there," Sandy said as he picked up one of the bags.

"That'll bring the cops," Jimmy said as he scrambled after Sandy who was already headed for the dividing fence.

"They don't want the cops to know what's in these bags."

"What now?" Jimmy asked as he and Sandy got in the front of his car after securing the two sports bags in the boot.

"I'd like to be here when they get back, but this car out the front all the time is obvious. I wonder if Steve would bring his car around?" Sandy thought aloud, and pulled out his mobile, he thought for a few seconds then pressed the ten numbers.

"Steve. Sandy. Good, listen Jimmy and I are at the Motel, these blokes are away at the moment and I wouldn't like to be found sitting in the same car out the front when they come back, because they are going to get one hell of a shock when they open their door." There was silence on Sandy's end while he listened.

"We broke in and took something," there was another block of silence, "you'll be here in five minutes did you say? Thanks Steve." He pressed the red button and looked at Jimmy.

"Would you mind taking the stuff back to your place when Steve gets here, I'll give you a call, we'll need all hands on deck to watch them once the shit hits the fan."

"What's in those bags?" asked Jimmy.

"Explosives."

"Back there?" Sandy's friend half turned and pointed to the boot.

"It's safe, it's got to be put together to go off. I'll guarantee the fellow in the Falcon with the interstate plates is the one responsible for last week's bombing on the Gold Coast."

"What do you think he intended to do with the stuff back here?" Jimmy asked as he indicated to the boot.

"Probably blow up the Sugar Bay."

"What!"

"I think they are capable of anything. They are looking at kidnapping charges and setting off a bomb on the Gold Coast at the moment, what's another boat. What is that treasure?"

Now it was Sandy and Steve, who were on surveillance duty. In the half hour they were together before the kidnappers returned Sandy filled his partner in on current happenings. The serious parts, Sandy's thoughts on the explosives, the Gold Coast bombings and the kidnapping, were somewhat lightened by the wrecking of the bathroom.

"The place will be flooded by the time they get back," Steve smiled.

"Here they come." Sandy had been patiently watching in the passenger side mirror. "I'll go for a walk you stay here." He walked across the road towards the reception office, he had an uninterrupted view of the front door of the forth unit down from the top, but would have been obscured by the office and a potted hibiscus by the door.

Derrick Fullerton with all his talk took charge again and hurried the Italians towards the front door. He pushed aside his captives and put the key into the lock, looked down and noticed water seeping under the door. He put his hand up commanding quiet, looked at the other three, as he hurriedly unlocked and opened the door. As he pushed the door in, the build-up of water washed over his shoes. He looked inside and saw that the two bags were missing. The two Italians were pushed inside while Bruno the bomber was sent for help.

Sandy took a couple of steps to his left out of the view of Brunno who was now running towards the office. The door opened and slammed, there were muffled sounds, some shouting and then three people came running out of the office towards the unit.

Sandy casually walked across the road in the direction of Steve's car and smiled to himself as he thought of the Motel Manager trying to cope with the explanation of the broken toilet suite, the cistern torn off the wall and water damage to the clothes that were left scattered all over the unit.

"The shit has hit the fan." Sandy smiled in glee.

The boys couldn't wait for their usual four o'clock drinks time to come around that afternoon. They had all eagerly done their surveillance duty and had the kidnappers in their sights who were now in their new digs, unit eleven, second floor of the Nelson Tower. That afternoon Sandy put a call through to that unit on the untraceable foyer phone at the Club before meeting the boys.

"Hello."

"Derrick Fullerton?"

"What?" Derrick couldn't pick the voice and a cold shiver went down his back.

"BANG!" Went Sandy.

Derrick Fullerton dropped the phone and ran to the window, the terror of uncertainty showed in his face. He looked across roof tops to the magnificent bay, the view holiday tenants pay good money for. Then this man who was now in Sandy's grip instinctively checked the bathroom even though they were on the second floor. The other three said nothing as they watched him come back to the wall phone which was left dangling and bashed it back onto the receiver; he tried to gather his composure.

"You. Get some takeaway," he scowled as he looked at Bruno.

"It's only a quarter past four!"

"Do it!" Derrick couldn't control the enemy, but he was giving the orders here. The two Italians looked at each other, there was some hope, and they knew Sandy was behind the chaos.

"What do you all feel like?" Bruno begrudgingly asked the Italians.

"Get anything and get out," the pressure was building, Derrick Fullerton was on a time contract with Ivan Sandvic and now he had to deal with someone he didn't know and who had the upper hand.

"Who is this Sandy Horder?" Derrick looked at the Italians expecting an answer. Muscat, was witnessing a man under pressure; he had seen it with his friend Dominic who was put in the same position by the man they now faced. And he no longer felt afraid. He had the confidence that someone was on their side.

"He is the man who saved Dominic and me; he is very brave, very strong."

"Yeah well he doesn't know who he's up against."

Muscat found some grit. He knew Sandy had this guy psychologically, he was the invisible man, he could see them, they couldn't see him. "He's got the explosives."

"Wadda you know about the explosives?" Derrick yelled.

"The two bags," Muscat said. "Sandy got them out of the Motel unit; we know your friend did the job on the Gold Coast," he pushed it a bit far, "you in deep shit."

"You shut up you, wait till the big ship comes in," he pointed to the heads, "then we'll see who's boss."

Downstairs in the underground car park Bruno walked to his Blue Falcon, there was a note on the windscreen which he didn't notice. While Jimmy was on surveillance duty he decided to set a trap of his own. He took the left rear wheel off the Falcon. Before he took the jack away Jimmy let the car down to its original height precariously balanced on two bricks, one on its edge the other lengthwise. The car rocked at the touch.

When Bruno arrived he unlocked the door and pulled it open. He didn't notice the slight rocking movement as all his attention was on the note on the windscreen, with a word written on the inside for the driver to see. He jumped in and strained forward to read the word in the poor light. The weight of the driver lifted the axel off the brick standing lengthwise in the opposite corner allowing it to topple. And then the car dropped unceremoniously to its hub.

There was a loud bump as Bruno read the word 'OOPS.' The explosives expert with the supposed nerves of steel ran across the car park and up the stairs to the unit. He slapped furiously at the door with his open hand; while a still shaken

Derrick Fullerton could only bring himself to look at the door.

"What?"

"Open up, open up!"

Derrick still physically on edge reefed the door open.

"What's up?"

"The car, she's on her side."

"What?" was all Derrick seemed to be able to say.

Muscat looked hopefully at his friend Dominic and grinned.

"Where's that bloody ship, we've got to get out of here."

"What ship?" Muscat whispered.

Derrick pulled Bruno inside and slammed the door, he pulled out a mobile phone pressed some digits and held it to his ear.

"You know who this is, where are you?" he listened.

"When will you get here?" he pressed the red button on the phone.

"Look at your contract Derrick Fullerton." The words of Ivan Sandvic came back to him, the four hundred thousand dollars up front was too good to knock back. Four months to deliver the goods seemed ample especially now that he had the location, but he had to deliver. You don't go back on a contract with Ivan Sandvic; 'The Sandman' puts you to sleep permanently.

CHAPTER 17

THE ESCAPE

"I had a good look at those explosives up at Jimmy's this afternoon," Steve said to Sandy over their drinks, "they have some big stuff there."

"I like the idea of the treasure, but this explosives business is a bit much I think," Walt always seemed to sit on the sideline.

"Yes you can get hurt with that stuff." His mate Dick wasn't far behind, he didn't find much use for explosives whilst selling real estate either.

"Hey boys we've got the bombs, not the crooks, when this is all over the cops will get an anonymous phone call as to where they can pick them up, in the meantime," Sandy went on, "it is out of harm's way."

"Yes these fellows haven't got anything to match what I've got if things get a bit hot" Maurice said.

"And what would that be Maurice?" Sandy asked.

"The old threeo I kept on the farm, she'll leave a fair hole in a tree stump."

"I don't want to hear about this," Sandy laughed.

"You could be fined for keeping that!" Walt looked accusingly at the old man.

"What's said at this table stays at this table," Sandy backed up the old man.

"Silence is golden." Jimmy seconded.

"We set out tomorrow at six, a morning's fishing, you fellows bring all your tackle, we could be watched, make it look normal. Steve and I will have some extra gear, we're going to look below," Sandy briefed the men.

"What, you and Steve?" Maurice asked.

"Just Steve," Sandy explained.

"Tomorrow night we could be rich!" The boy in Jimmy couldn't stay silent any longer. At the end of the last shout Sandy reiterated his words from last night.

"We will keep this to ourselves."

"Silence is golden." Jimmy seconded again.

There were two cabs at the front door of the Club when the men left, Sandy walked over to the one he recognized and let himself into the front passenger seat. "G'day Jeff."

"Sandy, where are you off to?"

"The little Italian place on Magnus Street."

On reaching his destination Sandy asked the driver for his card with his mobile number, "I'll give you a call later on." He paid the driver, got out and watched him go before heading towards the Nelson Towers.

He put his hand in his pocket and felt what he was looking for before walking to the entrance ramp of the underneath car park. From here Sandy could see a dozen cars including the Blue Falcon which seemed to be leaning to the left rear corner. Derrick's red car was not there. He felt the object in his pocket again and boldly walked up to the front door. There was nobody on the reception desk, so he moved quickly to the stairs. On the second floor he found unit eleven.

He quietly knocked and waited. A few seconds passed. He knocked again louder and waited, still no response. Sandy Horder looked both ways in the hallway to make sure that he was alone. He backed up to the wall opposite door eleven, put his shoulder down low, almost in line with the lock and charged. He was a solid man, his size and momentum busted the door open. Once inside Sandy picked up the small splinters of wood from around the lock and stuffed them in his pocket. The door knob and lock mechanism stayed intact, the keeper on the door jamb was the weak link, and the force broke it away together with three or four centimetres of timber. Sandy stepped outside pulled the door to and inspected the overall picture. It was passable.

Next he pulled the objects from his pocket, two small rolls of explosive wire, he wrapped the ends around the inside door handle, let about seventy centimetres hang down and stepped outside. He then pulled the door almost closed, leaving just enough room to get his hand inside and tie the two loose ends of wire around the inside light switch, thus giving the impression of a trip wire. Sandy inspected his work, wiped everything with a handkerchief and gently closed the door.

As he reached the bottom of the stairs Sandy saw Derrick and Bruno with the two Italians coming in through the front door. He immediately turned and retraced his steps to the second level and took refuge in a corner at the end of the hallway.

He listened as the ill-disposed voices approached. He risked a quick look around the corner and saw Derrick Fullerton's free hand go up as he tried to put the key into the lock. The unlatched door opened as far as the fake explosives wires would allow. "The joint's wired!" it was a mad man yelling, pushing every one out of his way scrambling to save himself. They all ran downstairs one by one yelling "Bomb, Bomb."

Sandy hurried to the door pulled the loose wires off the inside of the door handle, pushed them back into his pocket and wiped everything down again with his handkerchief and then made his way to the stairs.

The word bomb was echoing around the foyer as Sandy hastily found the front door under the cloak of catastrophe. His job was almost done. He had done irreparable damage to Derrick Fullerton's plan for the second time. Now he had to get the Italians away from him.

Sandy looked towards the entrance of the underneath car park when he came out onto the street and saw Derrick and Bruno with their two captives walking down the car park ramp, he hastened his step then ran. "Run Muscat!" he yelled as he passed the entrance to the ramp.

The two Italians swung around and saw their opportunity. Muscat grabbed his friend's arm and struggled with the rising ramp encouraged by Sandy's voice.

A shot rang out, in the poor light Sandy instinctively dropped and looked around. The two Italians stopped almost at the top of the ramp, freedom meters away. A second shot was fired. Sandy sighed a sigh of relief when the two Italians raised their hands.

Sandy had to do something, he needed back up because the captors would be making a run for it and the boys would be ruled out because of the afternoon drinking session.

He jumped to his feet and brushed the front of his shirt. "You alright mate?" A couple of window shoppers hurried out of the adjoining arcade. "It, it sounded like gunshots," Sandy the hero was playing the part of Clark Kent.

"I'll call the cops," an over helpful onlooker offered.

"Yes by all means," Sandy pulled out his own phone moved away, and took the card from his shirt pocket. "Jeff it's Sandy," he listened, "no I haven't eaten yet, can you pick me up from," he thought for a second, he didn't want to be at the scene of the crime, but he needed to watch, "opposite the Sea Breeze," it was one of the town's famous watering holes, cabs pulled up there all the time, and it had a good view of the car park.

He walked across the road keeping a watch on the car park entrance and headed for the pick-up point. A screech of tyres heralded the red car's appearance at the top of the car park ramp. Sandy unconsciously looked at his watch as if this would make Jeff's taxi arrive quicker. He could do nothing except watch the car go up the hill and take a left at the very top.

Jeff and his cab turned up a couple of minutes after Derrick's red car disappeared. "Where to Sandy?"

"Not sure," Sandy wasn't about to let Jeff in on the story so far.

"Can you go to the top of the hill and go left."

As they drove off people were gathering around the car park entrance.

"What's going on here?" the cabbie asked.

"Don't know," Clark Kent put on his unknowing, uncaring look.

"I went into the Sea Breeze to catch up with a bloke, he'd left. I'll catch him at home."

Sandy was giving the cabbie the impression of going to someone's place of residence, just then the radio cut in. "There's been a reported shooting at Nelson Towers all cabs in the vicinity respond."

"This is car two a bit of commotion in front of the car park, over."

"Any casualties, are the Police on scene? Over."

"No. I've got a fare to," the cab driver looked at Sandy.

"The Bowling Club," Sandy needed to find the red car. The Bowling Club was at the top of the hill. A siren was heard.

"Sounds like the cops," Jeff said into his hand-piece.

The street at the top of the hill ran up to the Bowling Club and further on to Golf Club, it wasn't a through road, only one way in and one way out. At the Bowling Club Sandy paid the cab driver and headed towards the front door of the Club, but only long enough for the cab to disappear. He knew these villains would drive into the Golf Club car park, realize they were trapped and tear back out the way they came in.

As he reached the road Sandy saw the lights coming over a slight rise at a pace. He judged his move in a second. He ambled out into the path of the speeding car, his escape route being the grassy bank on the other side of the road. Then like a drunk, looked at the lights, stepped back, then stepped out again this time running for safety of the grassy bank.

The brakes grabbed, the tyres screeched on the bitumen, four hands grabbed at the steering wheel as the speeding car jumped the gutter just past where Sandy took refuge.

"That bloody drunk, did we hit him?" Derrick looked at Bruno still gripping the steering wheel in a vice grip with a mad look in his eyes.

"I've killed him."

"You haven't killed anyone, get out of here."

"We can't leave him there I'll go and check," Bruno objected.

Derrick pulled the gun on Bruno yelling, "Get out of here."

"Let us go we won't say a word," Muscat pleaded for himself and Dominic.

"Shut up!" Derrick waved the gun around as he awkwardly turned in his seat to look at his two captives. He turned back to Brunno.

"Drive."

Sandy jumped to his feet when the car started again. The spinning wheels on the dew covered slopping bank had the car zigzagging back up to the road. Sandy grabbed at the rear passenger door handle opening it, but was knocked over by the erratic pendulum swing of the car's rear.

The interior light had everyone looking at the open door, then an arm disappearing into the darkness. "What the hell's happening?" Derrick was verging on madness as his car jumped the gutter again and back onto the road. "Close the bloody door," he screamed at Muscat. The Italian leaned over to his friend.

"Sandy" he whispered.

"Get out of here," Derrick was being overcome by this puzzling madness.

"The Motel was broken into, the unit was wired, now somebody is trying to get into the car, just go," he shouted. Bruno struggled with the wheel as he tried to accelerate once he was back on the road.

"What is wrong?" Derrick's tone was still at rage point.

"We must have blown a tyre when we hit the gutter."

Sandy watched the car with the shredded right front tyre limp up the road. Knowing they couldn't get far and couldn't go fast he cut down through the bush towards the main road back to the Bay. With extra strength and energy that a man seemed to be able to call on, he forged a track through the dark scrub land keeping an eye on the road above and the car for as long as he could. Will and determination got Sandy over a couple of miss footings until he went off the edge of a half meter drop, he instinctively grabbed his knees as he rolled over the low undergrowth and into a tree.

Sandy took stock. He felt the ripped arm of his shirt and the blood. He raised his arm a couple of times, superficial was his diagnosis. Instinctively he touched his breast pocket. "Oh no, not the phone!" it must have come out in the commando roll. Sandy looked up to where he had just come from. "I've got to have the phone." He got down on all fours and patted the ground, working his way back over the track he had made.

In a couple of moments his eyes became more and more accustomed to the darkness, however, not good enough to find a black phone in the night. Just then Sandy noticed a blue glow from his phone three or four meters to his left.

"Thank God for technology," he uttered as he dived for the light before it dimmed again.

It was ten minutes before Sandy saw lights again. He had been more cautious now and kept a hand on the phone in his pocket. He kept away from the street lights and hooded his eyes with his right hand to help maintain his night vision.

It paid off the red car was in an ill lit lane way at the side of a house half way down the hill back into town. Three men stood together while a fourth worked a jack on the right side of the car. Sandy had to get closer, he ran across the road stopped in front of the house on the corner of the lane way put two hands on the picket fence and vaulted into the front yard. His left foot got the edge of an old galvanized bucket under a tap; the opposite edge got Sandy on his shin. He grabbed at the excruciating pain and went into a commando roll for the second time that night. The metal bucket on the tap got a dog barking and shortly thereafter a verandah light came on. Sandy lay still, there were footsteps on the verandah and a dog's panting. "What is it old feller?" The dog barked again.

In the lane way at the sound of the bucket smashing and the dog's barking a harsh order was given. "Shut up." Sandy held tightly to his throbbing leg, whoever it was on the verandah and his foe on the other side of the fence were having a silent standoff. Each listening for a giveaway sound. The verandah contingent gave in.

"Good dog," there were footsteps, a door closed, the light went off.

Sandy crawled up to the inside of the fence, the voices were muffled but he heard Muscat.

"What are you going to do with us?"

"You are going to tell me where that treasure is," there was a pause, "tonight."

"Thanks to whoever your friend is every cop in town will be looking for us now, we'll lay low till morning by then the boat will be in and once we're on it we're safe."

"What boat?"

"The salvage boat, did you think I was waiting for the treasure to get washed up on the beach?"

"Uh?"

"You're gonna talk old fella, or I'll feed you both to the sharks."

Dominic sobbed and wet himself again.

"You go and help with the tyre," Derrick's whisper was a command to the Italian.

"Let him go he knows nothing," Muscat found some courage.

"So you do know where it is?"

"Yes, but I won't tell you until you let him go."

Derrick Fullerton lost it and struck Muscat with the gun on the cheek knocking him to the ground the whispering was gone. "If you don't tell me, I'll shoot you now."

"Every cop in town is at the bottom of the hill, if I die the grid references go with me."

Confidence and courage go together. Muscat grabbed the villain's leg and rolled with determination. Derrick fought for his balance but he fell heavily on his right elbow and squeezed off a single round before dropping the gun in the darkness.

On the other side of the fence Sandy was on his feet and hobbling towards the front picket fence, the dog barked and the verandah light came on once again.

In any fight fair or otherwise, surprise is the best punch. Sandy picked his friend up by the shirt collar with his bloodied arm saving the good right one for Derrick Fullerton who was struggling to get to his feet with a painful elbow.

"Get in the car," Sandy ordered as he hit Derrick in the eye with a short jab. "Is the tyre right?" he met Bruno who was at the back of the car and coming to help. "Too late son," and down he went. "Is the tyre right?" he asked again. This time Dominic recognized the voice.

"Yes Sandy, yes Sandy."

"What's going on? I'm calling the Police." It was a voice from the other side of the fence.

"Call them." Sandy was in charge again, behind the wheel of the red car. "Do up your seat belts gentlemen."

"Thank God, thank God," the two Italians muttered as they crossed themselves and could not believe the complete turnaround in the events that led up to this point.

"That's alright," Sandy brushed it off, "we have to get away from here and get rid of this car."

"What do you want us to do?" Muscat leaned forward in the back seat.

"I'll get us back to my place, store the car there for the night and leave it somewhere in the morning."

"They've got a salvage boat coming tomorrow!" Muscat exclaimed.

"Right," Sandy said, he had heard the conversation, "and it's no good to them if they don't know where to go."

"Yes," Muscat smiled in relief for the first time in two days.

Sandy did a wide loop around the earlier fracas on the way back to Shoal Bay and cut across the main road at the bottom of the hill. They got a quick glimpse of three Police cars blocking the main street and another speeding up the hill towards where they had just come from, no doubt responding to a reported gunshot minutes before.

"We're on fire," the happy Italian showed his white teeth again. "Those boys could be caught tonight."

Sandy agreed. "In the interim we'll get back to my place hide this car and go treasure hunting tomorrow."

"Sounds like a plan," Muscat looked at his relieved friend, "whatever you say."

They showered, Sandy found some clothes that almost fitted his friends and they still made it to the dining room before closing. "I would really appreciate it if my friends and I could eat at this unreasonable hour," the star guest said to the girl on the restaurant booking desk who also doubled as receptionist.

"It would be our pleasure Mr. Horder," she showed the men to a table overlooking the Bay.

"You sure got some style Sandy Horder," Muscat said "a three bedroom unit upstairs, this beautiful restaurant. Do you eat here every night?" he screwed up his fat face.

"Not every night."

"And that big cruiser out there?" Muscat went on, "I've been there," he shook his head. "It always comes undone with me."

'If only he knew,' Sandy thought, 'if only he knew the real story.'

CHAPTER 18

SUNKEN TREASURE

At six o'clock the next morning Sandy had the *Sugar Bay* tied up at the wharf. His rod was racked as if it was a normal fishing trip, then the troops came led by Maurice Campbell. He carried his rod in his left hand and seemed to struggle a bit with an old hessian bag tied at one end thrown over his other shoulder. Steve Flint and Jimmy Zininski each carried a large cardboard carton, no fishing tackle. Dick Walker and Walt McEnroe bought up the rear with the rest of the stuff.

"Boys" Sandy stood on the deck with his two Italian friends as he helped Maurice step over the gunnel and offered to take the bag.

"I'm right," the old man guarded the prize and offered the fishing rod instead.

The other two gave up their cardboard cartons even though they were not heavy, it was easier to board, and they in turn helped Walt and Dick with the extra rods.

"You all remember our two friends?" Sandy went on with the introductions. "We meet under different circumstances this time," he went on, "although we don't know what to expect out there."

A lot of handshaking followed; it was genuine comradeship, one team, and two goals, to find the treasure and to beat the enemy.

"OK Maurice what's in the bag?" Sandy laughed.

"The gun," he replied, "what's in the boxes?"

"Give me a look," Sandy smiled without answering the question.

The old man knelt and placed the hessian bag on the deck, he undid the thin rope which secured the open end and pulled out a long object wrapped in a white bed sheet. The crew gathered around in a circle to inspect this relic of the past.

Maurice stood up as he pulled the .303 from the shroud in a dramatic unveiling.

"Wow," Steve said as he reached out. "Do you mind?"

The proud old man handed the weapon to the retired military man who handled it with precision, the thumb checked the safety at the same time lifting and pulling back the bolt. He pointed the ancient piece towards the water, lifted it, tilted it to the left and looked down the barrel. "Beautiful." The way a gun fancier handles a weapon, the way a gun owner presents the weapon draws them to each other.

"I strip her and clean her every week."

"We are talking about the gun here." A playful Jimmy couldn't let the moment go.

The old man carried on, ignoring the remark and took a yellow absorbent cloth from the bag, he wiped the barrel again as he took the gun back from Steve. "Let's see your box of tricks," he said to Sandy.

Sandy checked the wharf. It was too early for the tourist types who usually take their stroll out to check the boats. He now knelt and opened a carton.

It was Steve again who stepped in. "This is serious stuff Sandy," he said picking up a cluster of cylindrical items.

"Careful" Walt put his hand out as a shield.

"Won't hurt ya," Jimmy assured Walt.

"What would you know?" Walt never had any faith in the man he referred to as the drunk.

"Steve and I went through it last night you gotta wire red to red 'n green to green. That right Steve?"

"Good Jimmy." He then went back to the serious conversation, he had handled explosives in the services and like everything Steve did, he was thorough and competent. Sandy smiled with confidence at the strong member of the team.

"As Jimmy said, we went through it last night. They had something for everything here."

Without handling anything else Steve pointed to various objects in the carton, the men looked closer. "There are assorted detonators, the ones in the green wrapping are not just waterproof but will work at any depth, could be handy on the sunken treasure."

"What's the trigger?" Sandy asked.

"This little thing?" Steve picked up a small stainless steel item similar to the stick in an ice block.

"Careful," Walt was edgy.

"Red to red 'n green to green," Jimmy considered himself Steve's assistant.

"Everything is double safety Walt, this device has to have a battery. The explosives have to be made active."

"What sort of a bang is in there?"

"Half of what's in this box alone would level," he stood up and looked to the shore, "the pub."

"That much?" Jimmy's mouth was wide open.

"Red to red, green to green son," Walt threw it back at the youngest member of the crew.

"We had better get this away and get out there," Sandy picked up one of the cartons, Steve's assistant the other. He followed Sandy through the hatch and down three steps. Between the bottom step and the entrance to the galley and bunks, chests had been built in, with padded tops so as they doubled as seats. Sandy opened the one on the right. "We'll put the cartons in here Jimmy."

"Ok, what's in the other one?" Jimmy always the little boy opened it. There was diving gear, tanks flippers, masks and belts.

"We're going under the waves," Sandy explained.

The *Sugar Bay* was almost to the heads when they spotted her. She was still a mile or so out but was headed for the same gap that Sandy and his boys were about to negotiate.

She was over sixty foot and seemed to have a large crane in the middle of the deck and a smaller one on the stern. The crew stood along the starboard side holding the rail, no matter what the outside sea was like the heads were always choppy. Sandy standing at the wheel picked up the binoculars.

"That's what they're waiting for," it was Muscat the big Italian who pointed "that's his salvage boat, he say, 'wait till the ship gets here.'"

Sandy put the binoculars down and looked at Muscat. He pulled the stainless steel lever at his right hand back slightly and lifted the bow.

In half an hour the *Sugar Bay* was at the spot idling in diminishing circles with Steve on the wheel and Sandy directing from the monitor next to him.

"Ok there she is." Sandy moved aside to give Steve a look.

"That's some boat!" Steve said.

Everyone looked at each other, the Italians hugged and jumped up and down. "Let's get the loot and get out of here" Jimmy exclaimed.

"If it were only that easy" Steve said looking again at the monitor, "it's not deep."

"What do you want to do?" Sandy looked at Steve.

"I'm going to take a look."

"Would you give him a hand Jimmy?" Sandy asked.

"I'm not going down there."

"With the gear," Sandy explained.

The mood was jubilant when Steve came up in all the gear. He had attached a rope to the diving belt and went through a basic procedure with Sandy.

"I'll pull once to let you know I'm there, twice to let you know I'm coming up. Three times if I think I've found something. Don't at any time try to pull me up."

He checked the tanks and valves tried the mask then slipped his arms through the shoulder straps and fastened the belt around his middle.

"Ok gents here we go." He sat on the gunnel and went backwards into the ocean.

The crew stood mesmerized at the railing as they watched. Sandy feed the communication rope down and down, there was a fear of the unknown, the same thoughts went through each of their minds. He was their friend, where had they sent him?

"The rope stopped." It was Sandy who broke the silence.

Everyone said to the man alongside of him. "The rope stopped."

There was one pull. "He's there!"

"He's there!" was echoed ten times, it was a relief.

Sandy heard the chopping sound seconds before he turned to see a helicopter coming in low over the starboard side. He was caught by surprise, the absolute sound and sight of something so big to come out of nowhere was terrifying, instinctively he hit the deck. "Get below!" He gave the order and chanced a look at the helicopter which was now going almost straight up and turning for another swing over the *Sugar Bay.*

The crew scurried for the hatch in a desperate race for self-preservation. Sandy prostrated himself alongside one of the railings while frantically hanging onto the communication rope.

The chopping of the blades out over a motionless boat on a still sea was deafening. The down draft so intense Sandy thought there would be a collision, he dare not move. In seconds the sound waned, Sandy chanced a look. The craft was a spot speeding away in the distance not twenty meters above the ocean. He was angry, this was trouble.

The hatch opened, Jimmy's head appeared, "You alright Sandy?"

"Yeah," A puzzled skipper looked back in the direction of Shoal Bay where he knew the helicopter was headed.

"What was that all about?" The youngest member of the crew asked as the others filed out dipping their heads on the top step with terrified faces and questioning.

Sandy said nothing.

"That bloody Derrick Fullerton, he never gives up, there something big down there," Muscat said pointing over the side.

Sandy looked at the rope in his hand.

"We'll see what Steve comes up with," he said trying to keep everyone calm on a boat an hour off shore.

Ten minutes went by Sandy looked at his watch he didn't think to ask how long those tanks can keep you down there. Another ten, everyone was getting edgy, nobody spoke.

There was a pull on the rope.

"Thank God! One, two, he's coming up, no three he's found something!"

"What do we do?" it was Jimmy who asked, as he looked towards the bay.

"We can only wait," said Sandy while holding the communication rope.

The wait seemed forever, but the crew knew the two best men were in control. There was another two pulls on the rope.

"He's coming up," Sandy was relieved.

Sandy and Jimmy helped Steve on to the back landing. The diver divested himself of his mouthpiece and mask, undid his belt and slipped the tank straps over his shoulders. He stood up and shook his head. "She's down there, she's big, she was a beautiful ship" Steve rubbed his right hand over his face.

"You are definitely onto something." Steve looked directly at Sandy. "Have a look at that." Steve pointed to a long metal object that he had placed on the back landing that no one noticed during their endeavours to get him on board.

The crew seemed not to be able to take in all that was presented to them. Here was a group of fishermen told not forty eight hours ago that they had been chosen to search for sunken treasure, had engaged an enemy on the ground and in the air and now this.

They looked at the object. It was at least two meters long with a large ball at the top of the tapered shaft. "I rubbed it in the sand to clean part of it," Steve said as he picked up the awkward top heavy object. He rubbed his hand over the part of the ball he had cleaned. It revealed a green stone the size of a tennis ball.

"That's an emerald!" Maurice Campbell exclaimed.

The men stood in silence, their eyes unblinking on the stone the colour of the sea. No one had seen nature so beautiful. Sandy reached out to examine the prize more carefully. "It's heavy" Steve said handing it to Sandy who rubbed his thumb around the stone next to it. He then took a handkerchief from his pocket, rubbed the top of the ball, and part of the long shaft.

"It's gold!"

"Is this what we came for?" Jimmy broke the silence after a minute.

"It's the first thing I picked up as a," Steve waved his hand around, "souvenir, there's stuff lying all over the place down there."

Every man handled the object rubbed it and uncovered more of its treasure.

"If that's solid gold it's worth a fortune," Walt said as he handed the prize onto Maurice who was standing beside him.

The old man examined the thing, held it up, ran his eye along its length, felt it a few times for weight then looked at Walt. "Walt, I think this could be worth more than a fortune," he thought and searched for the words to make credible what he wanted to say, "it's some kind of orb either religious or from some monarchy or realm."

"Where did you find it Steve?" Sandy Horder asked.

"On the deck, you see the boat itself is huge, there is nothing like it in Port Stephens. I just tried to get around as much of it as I could, and probably saw only half and that's only the deck I didn't go inside. There was stuff lying everywhere," he went on, "I just grabbed this on my way back up."

"I'd love to see it," Sandy mused.

"I've got to go back, especially after this," Steve pointed to his find.

In ten minutes Steve was suited up again, he tied the rope to his belt. "Are you right with that," he said to Sandy as he handed him the other end and tested his mouthpiece. They both nodded and Steve went over the side backwards.

"Why do they go in that way?" Jimmy queried.

"Because that's how they do it in the movies," it was one of only a few funny things Walt ever said to Jimmy.

The water was like crystal which visibility made the job a pleasure. Steve took in the creatures which swam around him and as he got closer to his objective he was able to appreciate the coral, the waving sea grass and vegetation.

Looking at the vessel now sitting perfectly still on the ocean floor Steve wondered how it could go straight down like that. Why wouldn't it roll in a wild sea? He could see no external damage. He swam over the lower deck where he'd picked up his find on the first dive which was one of seemingly countless objects and artifacts that seem to be strewn across the deck. He looked around and was drawn to the stairs that lead to the bridge. He glided over and up the narrow stairway.

Because he had approached the vessel from the stern on his two visits he wasn't able to view the bridge from above. A giant ray under the metal stairs momentarily grabbed his attention. When he looked up again a large bore gun lay across the bridge deck at the top of the stairs. Steve gasped on his mouthpiece, and then his eyes still at deck level looked straight across at the skeletal remains sitting under the wheel. He grabbed his mouthpiece in a state of panic.

Some minutes passed. Steve looked everywhere but at the skeleton until he felt his heart rate ease back he found two more skeletons on the bridge. One clutched a machine gun the other lay near an open door.

Steve swam over and pushed the door, the top hinge and the architrave gave away showing access to a vertical timber stairway. He swam back over to the bridge rail and attached the communication rope to it, he needed to be unhindered.

He then swam back to the broken door and headed down, it was dark. Just to the right at the bottom of the staircase he felt a large desk. Moving around the walls he found a door, and with a push it gave away like the one at the top of the stairs. 'Probably a bedroom.' Steve guessed that he was in the office with a staircase leading straight up to the bridge. 'This is probably the master's suite. There would be a door opening on to the deck that would allow some light in. Right again Steve, pull this door in.'

The shark had just passed the door when it sensed movement and with a flick of its tail, its snout was at the open door. Steve froze. The bubbles from his dislodged mouthpiece had the shark ramming the doorway. Some light spilled into the suite as Steve back peddled to the opposite wall. 'Keep him out or he will kill you,' Steve yelled at himself.

He had backed up to the desk, instinctively he felt around behind himself. His fingers touched a metal handle, intuitively his hand wrapped around it and then he swam frantically towards the monster with his weapon raised above his head. It was kill or be killed as this beast smashed away at the opening.

Steve landed his best strike first, brandishing the twelve inch broad knife with the diamond encrusted handle. It, like the emerald embedded orb now on the *Sugar Bay* up top, was a ceremonial object. It now tore at the left eye of this grey beast and had it as mad as hell. Its head reared up smashing the timber work above the door right to the ceiling dislodging the ceremonial object from Steve's hand in doing so. Steve grabbed the floating weapon and thrust it deeply into the underbelly of the killer beast and with panicked strength tore a wound as long as his arm.

The shark retreated. The huge gash drained the life blood from the sleek once powerful body. It went almost listless through the starboard railing Steve headed for the communication rope, gave it two frantic pulls and headed up.

It took Sandy and the strength of the two Italians to pull Steve onto the back landing with all his gear. Exhausted he couldn't help them and he wasn't letting go of his knife. Sandy flicked the straps on the tank, did the same with the belt and slipped off his friends face mask before lifting him onto the main deck.

"You OK?"

"Give me a minute."

The crew stood around in a tight circle, the diver wasn't marked in any way but there was shock in his face, they knew he had a story to tell.

It was three minutes before Steve sat up, he looked at the old man. "Check that out Maurice," he held the knife up. Maurice took a handkerchief from his pocket and rubbed the handle.

"They're diamonds," he said in a low disbelieving voice. The creases between his eyes deepened.

"What happened down there?" It was Sandy who spoke when he saw the blood on Maurice's handkerchief.

Steve looked up at Sandy "There are sharks down there."

"There was a fight?" Sandy asked.

"To the death," Steve got to his feet.

"Look I don't know how that boat ended up like it did," he looked at Sandy, "I think there was a gunfight down there, there must have been a rebellion of some kind" Steve added.

"S--h--i--t," Jimmy strung it out for five seconds.

"There will be bloodshed and it won't be the sharks," Muscat warned. "Men would kill for the two items we've already got."

Sandy disregarded the Italian.

"What else did you see?" he looked at Steve.

"There were three skeletons on the bridge a shotgun, a machine gun and a pistol snub nose. I didn't get to the bridge on my first dive and when I saw this," he went on "I started to investigate, that's when the shark came in."

There was silence.

"I think," Steve said "they brought the boat down with a rebellion."

"Maybe some of the crew didn't think taking the boat to Sydney was a good idea, or maybe they wanted to keep it all for themselves and steer it into Newcastle or somewhere," Sandy said.

"Yeah," Steve wasn't convinced. "How did it go straight down like it did? You know there was a fight, down there nobody won."

Can I see the dagger?" Sandy asked. "What would you clean this up with Maurice?"

"Vinegar, white vinegar," he replied.

The object passed through eight sets of hands. "All these small bumps are diamonds?" Walt asked. "It must be worth a fortune."

"Look at it this way Walt," Maurice said, "the diamonds on that knife and the emeralds on the orb identify them as a particular part of a treasure from another time and another place. Their material melt down value would be worth a fortune" he agreed "but the unique collection no matter how big would be incalculable."

The words stayed with Sandy Horder. Derrick Fullerton and his bomber mate from the Gold Coast were the men he was dealing with. How would they know about ancient artifacts being smuggled out of Asia and what was the origin of this stolen haul? And it was stolen because cheap crooks and bombers were trying to steal it again. Sandy was feeling a bit like the treasure police, he was going to find it and give it back to history. It felt good. It felt real good. It would even up the balance.

"Sandy, Sandy," he was so deep in his own self-righteousness he didn't hear Jimmy, "what's the plan?"

"We'll secure these items until we get the lot."

"Where?" Jimmy asked.

"Here on the boat."

"You said they were irreplaceable."

"We'll guard them around the clock."

"Let's go back in." Sandy concluded as he headed up the three steps to the wheel.

"It's easily achievable." Maurice joined Sandy and Steve up at the wheel.

"You reckon Maurice?" Sandy gazed ahead, one hand on the wheel.

"Of course," the old man answered. "I mean you found it just like that, it's a mere three quarters of an hour off the coast, we go down and bring it up."

"What about the sharks?" Steve put in.

The old man knew when to say nothing. After all he wasn't the diver.

"Maurice," Sandy said, "Steve and I have been talking, those blokes back at the Bay are bad, they have a salvage boat and they want this stuff. They need the co-ordinates, they know we have been out today," he went on. "We are all in danger of being grabbed for those grid lines."

"I don't know what they are," Maurice was defensive.

"They will think you are lying," Steve said. He knew that they were in a spot. They had to work this through.

"What are we going to do?" Somehow Maurice knew Sandy would come up with an answer.

"Well," Sandy started as he waved the others up from the deck. "Men we have got to get ready for when we get back. Our friends will be waiting with their salvage boat, as I was just saying to Steve and Maurice here they have everything but the co-ordinates, so we must be vigilant. They really only know Muscat and Dominic. They associate me only with this vessel although I have caught glimpses of them twice they were too busy both times to sight me."

"Tell us what we need to do," Muscat would go anywhere with Sandy.

"We'll kick this around. Once we're in through the heads we take a wide birth around Shoal Bay and head up to the Soldiers Point Marina. You all get your wives to pick you up, I'll stay on board."

"What about us?" Muscat was ready to do anything.

"You both stay with me."

"Our wives are going to want to know about the change of the mooring." Dick protested.

"Tell them nothing. Jimmy how about you ask your wife to pick you all up and drop the others off?" Sandy knew Jimmy's wife Isa didn't have anything to do with the other wives. It was a class thing. Wives of retired professional men and the wife of the cleaner! He smiled to himself. Emit Horsley wouldn't rate at all.

Sandy looked at the crew. "Not a word."

CHAPTER 19

PUTTING ON A SHOW

The next morning two lone figures sat in a rental car in front of the Country Club overlooking the Bay. "What did you do about the other car?" Bruno asked of Derrick Fullerton.

"I told them it was stolen," Derrick's manner was not favourable.

"There was nothing in it was there?" Bruno wanted to be reassured.

"No there was nothing in the bloody thing. In case you weren't watching that bloody super hero Sandy Horder pinched it. Now where is that boat of his?"

Derrick had been living on his nerves since he hit this magnificent water paradise. Every move he made was covered by this bloody Sandy Horder.

"We didn't see them come in. The boat is not at its mooring. They must be still out there." Bruno concluded.

Derrick shook his head. These people are out there pulling up this great treasure and he is paying fifteen hundred a day for the salvage boat to sit idle at Nelson Bay. He doesn't know where to start looking for these guys to get the coordinates to get hold of the treasure and time was ticking away on the contract.

He got out of the car and slammed the door. He had to get his thoughts together. He walked over to a picnic table sat down and looked over the Bay. 'Ok I need to one, kidnap one of Sandy Horder's people and get the information out of him? Now, the only people we know of Sandy Horder's are the Italians, you can be sure he has them well hidden given his resources. Or, two, we can wait until they bring the haul up and just take it? Nah, you can't just sneak up on someone out in the ocean, and grab the loot.' This was one hell of a dilemma.

In the meantime, Sandy warned his faithful crew "Tell them what you have to, but don't tell them the truth," as they left the boat and filed along the boardwalk to Isa in the waiting car in the car park at the Soldiers Point Marina.

"Why you change mooring from Shoal Bay?" Jimmy's wife Isa asked in her broken English as the four men climbed in.

"Don't worry about it love," was the way Jimmy dealt with Sandy's instructions. "I'll need the car tomorrow to come back here."

"Why here?" his wife thought she was entitled to an answer.

Jimmy ignored the question.

The three men in the back looked at each other with frowns of disbelief. No more was said.

At six a.m. the next morning the *Sugar Bay* left Soldiers Point Marina. It was cool, just breaking day.

"No hard questions at home?" Sandy asked Steve on the bridge as he turned his prized vessel into the main channel.

"No, quiet day on the water," Steve replied "said we had to come and try again."

He fiddled with the dial on the radio which connected all pleasure craft back to Marine Rescue, besides giving up dated forecasts it was a good tracker for boats lost at sea. Just give them your intended co-ordinates.

"When you get them, give them this one," Sandy pointed to a crossed line in the screen which was a mile or so from the treasure.

"That'll trick them if anyone is listening," Steve smiled.

"And keep an eye in the sky," Sandy was covering his tracks.

The sun had inched up well above the horizon and knotted up a couple of degrees when Steve declared that they were at the spot.

"OK boys grab the rods."

"Why, are we gonna pull it up with fishing lines?" Jimmy joked.

"No we are going to put on a show," Sandy answered.

Steve grabbed the rail and jumped the three steps from the bridge, while Sandy shut things down.

It was almost an hour before Steve announced from his position on the port side. "Someone was listening and here they come." The chopper was low. It wasn't looking for them it had their position from the Marine Rescue broadcast. This was a warning, they knew the position.

"Just keep fishing boys," Sandy ordered.

"They think we're putting on a show for them, and we are really looking below the waves for treasure."

"And?" Jimmy asked.

"We are putting on a show for them, because they think, we think, they know we're watching them watch us."

"What?"

"You learn that at Captain's school Jimmy." Steve explained.

The chopper went straight up as it did yesterday when it reached the boat, this time criss-crossing several times on the longitude and latitude lines, banked heavily for a good look then headed back.

"Don't look up," Sandy instructed "let them think they've got us."

"They think, we think," Jimmy laughed.

"Pull them in boys, we'll move onto the treasure."

In a half an hour Sandy slowed the hefty motors and idled the Sugar Bay into position. Steve gave the signal and tuned in the visual finder.

"Walt and Dick start the covering, Jimmy bring the diving gear up."

From the bridge Sandy oversaw the operation. Walt and Dick tied a green tarpaulin either side on the chrome railing, pulled it right over the bridge and tied it to the railing half way down the deck.

"Great idea Sandy," Steve praised, "it breaks up the outline of the ship. It blends in with the ocean you wouldn't see us from a mile off and when they get to the other site they will be more than a mile off so we've got all day to explore."

The old salvage ship ploughed through the heads into a moderate swell. She wasn't the type of craft that would attract a second glance with her dull, dark red undercoat, unfinished paint job, enhanced by large dabs of grey Galmet covering welded patches on an already pock marked exterior. Her large gantry of cranes fore and aft, scattered diving cages and chains together with an untidy crew said she was a working boat. At the heart of this well-worn beast was a completely refurbished ex-navy cruiser twin turbo power plant that could drive her and everyone on board to hell, if the Captain so desired.

CHAPTER 20

THE DIVE

Captain Gunnar Hagen was a big unshaven unsavoury Norwegian who lived on the salvage boat. The sea was his home. The ship and master knew each other. Their gruff exteriors indeed complimented each other.

Gunnar ran his tongue around the inside of his mouth as was his habit when he was concentrating. He was looking at the navigation screen, occasionally he looked up, for the second time he adjusted the course using a keyboard. Eventually he brought the power up to eighty percent.

The door to the bridge opened, one of two passengers bumped either side and almost fell with uneven footing as he stumbled in. "Are we in this much of a hurry?" Derrick Fullerton almost fell again as he struggled with both the forward thrust and side roll.

"I run this ship," Gunnar turned slightly, touching the ceiling to steady himself.

"We can hardly stand up out there," Derrick almost fell again when he let go of the shelf he was holding to steady himself.

"Go below," Gunar instructed as he turned to look forward again at the waves crashing over the bow, the conversation was over.

"How long before we get there?"

The sea fell away as the deck moved again and threw the passenger against the only door in the small room. He opened it and fell out onto the deck.

"Madman" Derrick murmured as the bridge door slammed behind him.

"Don't argue with him mate," a rough looking seaman in old ill-fitting clothes and rubber boots said gesturing toward the bridge window. "You could end up swimming home."

****

STEVE WAS SUITED up and ready to go.

"You sure you're right with this?" Sandy asked.

"I'm right now I've got this," the diver said holding a powered spear gun. He chewed on the mouthpiece and pulled the mask down then dropped off the gunnel.

Steve looked around, just a few small schools of fish, a lazy ray and the vast blue yonder. There she was lying as he left her, sitting on the sea bed. Steve smiled. Two safe havens, the *Sugar Bay* above and the cruiser on the sea floor. The tricky bit will always be the unguarded strip in between. He headed for the huge hole in the deck that would have covered the engines. It was empty. The bottom was blown out of the boat and the propeller shafts were bent and turned into the sea bed. If there had been an explosion and there clearly had been, then why didn't the whole thing go up? It blew the bottom out of the vessel. The Captain must have, therefore, pre-set the explosives around the engine bay as an assurance against any rebellious activity. At the onslaught of mutiny the Captain must have relayed his coordinates to someone before this giant vessel was sent straight to the ocean floor with all hands on board.

Steve headed for the bridge and the staircase direct to the Captains suite. He tied the communication rope to the wheel and slipped straight down the rotting staircase.

Once inside, through the clear water Steve checked the door, no sharks. He moved around the walls, there were deteriorating timber frames and stands, unrecognizable metal shields and plaques and other keepsakes you would find in a man's office. Not what we're looking for Steve assessed.

As he investigated every nook and cranny he manoeuvred himself behind the desk and pulled the handle on the top drawer, the face of which came off in his hand. Carefully Steve picked up a steel rule from the desk and felt inside the dark drawer. He felt a few objects and slid them out.

He knew what was in the two black bags tied at the top before they floated to the floor splitting and divulging one of man's coveted spoils. He gently pulled the drawer out. There were sixteen bags of diamonds. Steve could hardly contain his excitement. He grabbed two vases from the desk and put the gems into them for safe carriage to the top. Then he picked up the gun and checked it, took one last look for sharks and swum up the staircase to the bridge. He put the two vases on the deck and gingerly poked his head out of the hole and looked around.

All clear he pulled the rope twice and started the ascent.

Steve, with all the safety training that he had received over the years now had safety in his DNA. Cover every situation with a plan and a counter plan. Make sure nothing will go wrong before undertaking a mission.

With an ancient vase full of diamonds under each arm, Steve held the charged spear gun cocked and ready across his chest. He swam slowly straight up towards the underside of the hull of the *Sugar Bay* which would come into his view in the next few seconds.

The shark came from the port side of the wreck as if it had been waiting for its prey to swim into open water. A flick of its tail had the monster gliding straight up.

Maurice Campbell the old farmer, even though he loved to fish, knew nothing of diving and saw only danger in this exciting new venture. He stood on the bridge under the blue green tarpaulin with his trusty big bore .303.

There was excitement at the rear of the boat.

"He's coming up," Jimmy saw the rope pull twice on Sandy's hand.

Steve saw the bottom of the boat, he wanted desperately to show the boys his prize, and he soaked up the premature glory, and revelled in the praise that awaited him.

The old man was looking down towards the rope when he saw the ten to twelve foot shadow moving swiftly towards it. He raised the gun, grabbed the bolt, pulled it back lifting the round and drove it back with intent, shoving the solid point into the chamber. Slowly and deliberately he lined the ball at the end of the barrel with the gap in the V closest to his eye. He aimed at the head.

"BANG!"

Captain Gunnar Hagen, stepped out of the bridge onto the small landing of his salvage boat, he looked starboard as the loud gunshot reverberated around them, he picked up what he thought was the source and reached inside the bridge for his binoculars.

"What was that?" Derrick Fullerton and Bruno were up on deck.

The Captain gestured quietness with his right hand as he scanned the horizon. The noise faded.

"That wasn't far off," the Captain said not taking his eye off the spot from where he reckoned the shot came. "You" the Captain pointed to the young fellow he had in the bridge moments before. This surly disliked individual got things done with his frightening manner, not unlike Derrick Fullerton. "Get up on that crane," he handed the young deckhand the glasses, "tell me what you see about a quarter starboard."

The youngest crew member put the binocular strap around his neck and scrambled up the crane ladder.

"What is it?" the Captain roared.

"There's nothing there," the deckhand said almost apologetically.

"If I come up there son, you'll be comin' down, and not the way you went up," the Captain threatened.

Fear again brought an outcome. "Wait a minute, there's something like green out there."

'That explains it' the Captain thought. The shot came from that direction. But a green boat, he hadn't seen a green boat since he arrived three days ago, let's see what's going on.

He swung into the cabin, set a rough course and fired up the engines. The kid on the crane looked down. The cranky Captain leaned out of the bridge door and looked up. "Get down."

"What's going on?" Derrick pushed the bridge door open and demanded.

"We're moving to the right spot."

"But you said these were the co-ordinates, the treasure is down here."

"Well look at the screen, there is nothing down there. We've been had. I want to find this as much as you do," the grumpy Captain pointed just off starboard. "These blokes are on it, and they're cunning."

At the same time Steve Flint felt the vibration from the big bore gun just before he broke the surface, instinct swung his head to the left as the grey nurse shark felt the pain. The powerful forward motion stopped instantly the wide jaws posed no threat as a spout of blood sprung above the right eye. Fear grabbed Steve, his muscles contracted around the vases under his arms, his body stiffened as he got a shot off into the already dead beast.

On the deck it was the shot that alerted the crew to the danger below. There was terror in Steve Flint's eyes as he broke the surface. He spat out the mouthpiece. "Quick take the vases from me."

Jimmy pulled Steve's now free hand around to the loading step at the rear and dragged him on board. "Give me a minute," Steve lay on the deck exhausted, the encounter with the shark had his heart pounding in his chest. Walt and Dick joined Jimmy and Sandy around the wasted diver. The two vases rolled around the deck.

The old farmer pulled the tarp back from the bridge to make his descent.

"We've got company he called out and pointed to the salvage boat obviously at full power a mile or so off port."

Sandy jumped to his feet, he didn't have the elevation to see the distance the old man had but he sensed the risk of giving the location away. "Jimmy help Dick pull the tarp down, Walt stay with Steve. Come down Maurice." There wasn't room for two on the bridge stairs.

Sandy twisted the key and pulled the power down. The *Sugar Bay* lurched forward like the '52 Holden with its lightened flywheel and competition clutch. The two vases rolled to the back of the boat. Steve stretched and collared them both. Jimmy and Walt scrambled to keep their footing in the mad rush forward; it was the tarpaulin they were taking down that kept them upright.

Sandy instinctively swerved wildly out to sea in an effort to take attention away from the spot he had left. It worked. The Captain of the salvage naturally averted his attention to the reckless display put on by Sandy, as he tried to pick up his bede.

"Put one into the air Maurice," Sandy said to the old man standing at the foot of the stairs.

If Captain Gunnar Hagen's full concentration wasn't diverted slightly by the sudden take off of the *Sugar Bay* at first, the shock of a second gunshot had him pull his boat off course under manual mode. "Damn him!"

"We had the spot," Derrick Fullerton said.

"No, they let us think we had the spot." The Captain was mad that he had lost the bede he had on the diving location.

"How do you know that wasn't the spot," Derrick pointed back.

"What do you think this is for?" the Captain thumped the top of the square blue screen with his right hand.

"I've been looking at it for ten minutes there's nothing there. That's the *Sugar Bay* ," the Captain indicated with a lost stare, he shook his head. "They'll head back to port, he's cunnin' that one. If you want the right co-ordinates," Gunnar advised, "you'll have to get it out of him, one way or another."

"Where were they?" It was a so near yet so far question.

There's the ocean," Captain Gunnar Hagen held out his hand palm up, he had been beaten by a cleaver operator, "pick a bloody spot." The two men eyed each other. Derrick Fullerton wanted to belt this bloody arrogant Norwegian pig. He stopped, remembering one of the seaman's words 'don't argue with him, you could end up swimming home.'

"We know roughly the spot, could we search an area?" Derrick asked.

"We're closer to it than we were a minute ago, but in another minute we might have passed it."

"Stop here." Derrick yelled.

The Captain rough and tough as he was took the order, after all this dick head was paying the bills.

"Let's say we are within a mile of the spot, can we do a though search using this thing?" Derrick pointed to the screen. The Captain looked at the screen then back at the paying passenger without saying a word. These men were of the same temperament, anything could trigger them. They were dangerous. Derrick was careful, even though he was paying the bills this man scared him.

"How long?

"One, maybe two square miles," the big Norwegian roughly calculated. "Three, four days."

"Let's do it."

CHAPTER 21

THE STAR OF MIKONOS

Sandy Horder kept his craft full throttle headed due east for obscurity when Jimmy Zininski rushed up on the bridge. "Sandy you've got to come and see this," his eyes were wide, his words were rushed.

"What?"

"Quick!"

Sandy immediately pushed the twin throttles back and the big boat slumped forward. The three older members of the crew were huddled around Steve Flint on the deck at the rear of the boat. What was it? Sandy's first thought was Steve's well-being, such was the panic.

Walt turned from his crouched position and looked up at Sandy there was disbelief in his eyes. This reinforced Sandy's initial thoughts. Steve unfurled his hand. There were little tied bags around the diver on the deck. Nobody spoke.

The boat had stopped, the firing had stopped, and all was quiet. The two Italians came out from below and saw the huddle. Sandy was at one with the crew. They were mesmerized Steve sat on the deck a small black opened bag in one hand and a mint in diamonds in the other.

Muscat pushed his way between Walt and Jimmy kneeling on the deck, he smiled at the small recognizable bags that lay on the deck he knelt and touched several then picked up one.

Still kneeling he undid the rotting cord carefully and tipped the contents into his hand. "This is what they come for. They will kill for."

As if Sandy and his crew hadn't already overdosed on excitement, they were now subject to an intense heart stopping experience. "Good God!" Maurice exclaimed. One single diamond almost covered Muscat's hand.

"The Star of Mikonos," Muscat held it up expertly between his thumb and fore finger.

"Don't drop it," Dick implored.

The Italian let it fall. It hit the deck and rolled.

"It has been around for a long time my friend," he laughed the laugh of a man who knew the story. "Hard as diamonds."

Sandy looked around, he took two steps to the railing, he had to catch his breath and he had to keep the crew safe from the salvage vessel that had their scent. He felt vulnerable, as was the cruiser that was now sitting on the ocean floor. There was nowhere to go, no one to come to the rescue. Anything could happen out here.

"We're going in." Sandy announced, he beckoned Muscat onto the bridge, the rest of the men handed the diamond around. Sandy took a wide berth around the treasure area, he and his companion kept a sharp lookout on the starboard horizon.

"I see something," Muscat indicated.

Sandy grabbed the glasses. It was bigger than a fishing boat.

"Is that her?"

"Could be."

"I wonder if they are on the spot," Muscat thought aloud.

"They'd have to be lucky."

"If we had their gear, we could clean that spot up in a day," the Italian said.

"What?" Sandy leaned on the speed lifting the bow some.

"You saw what we are dealing with, small precious, cache. It's not like bringing up the sunken boat, that's only worth scrap anyway," Muscat hesitated. "Those diamonds Steve held in his hand would be worth millions."

"And the big one?" Sandy cut in.

"It's a name diamond, if that were to go to Sotheby's, buyers would come from all over the world."

Sandy could see his friend with a far-away look in his eye knew more than he had told them. "It's more than that. The Star of Mikonos is the centre of trove De La Constance." The Italian laid out his European accent deliberately.

"This is more than just a big deal?" Sandy tried to put it in layman's terms.

"When we heard it was on its way down from Hong Kong back in '97 we were all on alert. The Skipper of the sunken cruiser paid three million just for it, something to out run the pirates if need be. My cousin," Muscat went on "who owned the Marina in Queensland, told me, 'she won't stop here Muscat. They'll keep going and moor off Sydney, take the stuff in during the night.'"

Sandy looked at his companion on the bridge. He knew his own secret was big, now he seemed to be mixed up in history. "This trove......," Sandy didn't have the name.

"Trove De La Constance, is the treasure of the Catholic Cathedral of the same name in the south of France." Muscat informed him.

"Oh."

Muscat laughed, like all Italians he loved to tell stories, and his was a beauty. "Catholics are good people, well they tell you they are," the Italian corrected himself, "money changes everyone and the big story is how the Catholics came by this hoard."

In the late eighteen hundreds the square rigged trade ships would battle seasonal rough seas to get their merchandise up from Morocco to the ports on the Portuguese coast to be dispersed into Europe. It was a lucrative business, exotic cloths and tapestries, fascinating teas and essences, extravagant silverware and china and of course the contraband.

The ancient valuable relics from the old world that had been pilfered through ongoing wars over the centuries, irreplaceable artifacts that would eventually find their way into the kingdoms and palaces of Europe, were the prizes the Pirates would lay in wait off the Moroccan coast for. Neither rough seas nor canon could deter them for these ancient gems. They hunted down their prey like weak animals, took the most prized of the goods and then sent the rest and the crew to the ocean floor. This thieving scurrilous bunch of nomads lived in caves and humpies along the coast. There were no ethics there was no fear.

Fishermen liked the waters off the Straits of Gibraltar and those who ventured further into the open waters were rewarded handsomely for their envied catch. These men were the gallant gladiators of their day. They were big hard men who fought game fish with special nets and tangled with pirates who considered everything in the ocean theirs.

When these two groups met it was hand to hand, toe to toe. The fishermen didn't mind a good brawl and when they won, they took the pirate ship and everything on her leaving the scurrilous thieves looking up from the sea bed.

The irony in all of this was the pilfered priceless artifacts, or fruits of war, had moved through so many dishonest hands that the rightful owners, now so ancient would be unidentifiable and irrelevant.

The Trove De La Constance was the consequence of such a battle at sea, won by the fishermen. They were all good hard working Catholic men. When they returned to their home port on the Mediterranean French coast in their newly acquired pirate ship, they went to the most revered being in their town. The Bishop.

This holy man, God's representative in the community and supreme pastor of the Cathedral De La Constance, gave judgment on the hoard. It was decreed to be of no one person or persons advantage and thus to be hidden in a newly created crypt under the Cathedral.

Over the years The Trove De La Constance was shelved under mythical legend, but old timers who sat around their beautiful harbour sipping coffee would tell how their grandfathers saw the treasure and its centre piece which became known as The Star of Mikonos, so named by the Greek fisherman who led his men on that glorious day.

"So I've been chosen to see the Star of Mikonos," Sandy smiled and pulled the levers right back. He loved the sense of speed on a moderately calm ocean.

"A more righteous person I could not pick," the Italian gave all the praise to the sea Captain who found the treasure.

"What is it doing now off the coast of Australia after hiding under a church in the south of France for a hundred and fifty years?" was a good question.

"The war, the atrocities of war," Muscat looked away. "I wasn't even born, but I listened to the stories of my father and my grandfather. They saw Europe bombed, devastated. They saw the Nazis looting the ruins of our great cities and steal our treasures," he smiled. "Then the Americans came to saved us and then they stole it from the Nazis, but my friend," Muscat looked at Sandy. "They couldn't get it home."

"So how come it's here?" Sandy asked again.

"The Americans hid stuff all over Europe with the help of locals, to be retrieved after the war."

"And?" Sandy enquired.

Muscat Farincini laughed aloud. "The locals retrieved it, sold it to the highest bidder."

"You're kidding."

"The Asians are smart business people they bought tons of contraband and smuggled it to China, a lot of it ended up in the Philippines as well."

"I've heard of that," Sandy was intrigued, it made sense.

"A lot of Asian dictatorships flourished with the aid of our heirlooms, because of this and population growths, the world power is shifting east." Muscat showed small insights into basic economics.

"And it got here?" Sandy persisted with his question hoping to get a name or a time in history.

"Thieves are thieves, rumours get around," Muscat waved his arms around as he did. "Somebody heard the cruisers were stopping over on the Gold Coast at the start of this thing. Our friend got ready to steal the stuff. But," his arms started again "someone and someone big, told him. This is a big thing my friend," the Italian looked away again.

"What would you like to see happen to the Trove De La Constance?" Sandy had both hands on the wheel and looked ahead.

"I would like to see it go home," Muscat was of heavy heart, he could only picture the ruins of Europe, but he saw the unmistakably greed and lust in Derrick Fullerton's eyes, and that was only a dim reflection of the pain, suffering and death that this hunt for wealth had caused.

CHAPTER 22

LAYING LOW

Sandy trained the glasses on the large vessel to the starboard horizon. He guessed rightly that they would be scanning the depths with their radar gear.

At the same time, Gunnar Hagen looked in the direction where he knew the *Sugar Bay* would be. He knew they would head back to port, to safety. This coarse, raw, tragic old salt knew what to do. Find the boat and the skipper. He would enjoy the next bit.

The coast line was in full view and the gap was looming with Sandy alone now on the bridge and holding full throttle on a slightly adjusted course. He would drop the boys off at the Shoal Bay Wharf and take the *Sugar Bay* around to Soldiers Point at the other end of the water way for safe keeping.

"OK we'll get onto a mooring up around Soldiers Point and keep guard on all of this until our next outing," Sandy organized, he would take the two Italians with him. "You fellows carry on as normal."

"What about your place at the Country Club?" Jimmy pointed out. "Won't they wonder where you are?"

"I'll give them a ring."

It was three days before Jimmy noticed the salvage boat back in the calm waters of Shoal Bay. He knew they had found nothing, they were here to extract information and the only people they could finger were the two Italians on the *Sugar Bay* with Sandy. He immediately rang Sandy with his mobile.

"They're back," he sang "must have come last night."

"Thanks, good work Jimmy."

"What do you want us to do?"

"Ask Steve to come over to the Soldiers Point Marina, you come with him," there was a hesitation, "bring the explosives."

Back on the salvage boat things had become untenable. On the second afternoon of the treasure hunt at sea, (the) Captain Gunner Hagen in a mad fit of rage threw Derrick Fullerton off the bridge literally when the latter insisted on searching his way.

"I've paid for this expedition. You will see it out," Derrick threatened the salvage Captain as he picked himself up from the deck.

"There's just enough money there to get you back to port."

Derrick Fullerton and Bruno were unceremoniously kicked off the salvage at the Shoal Bay Wharf without a word being spoken. Gunnar then headed out into the bay to anchor and plan his move, he had a feeling about this treasure and the answer to its where-abouts was with Sandy Horder.

"We've got to find Sandy Horder," Derrick was enraged, time was running out, he didn't have a boat and he had made another enemy.

"It's a small town," Bruno didn't say much, he wasn't game. "Not many people got boats." The grammar wasn't good but he was right.

Derrick looked at Bruno then out to the still waters of the bay. "Gunnar would be watching all the movements on the water, I'll search the land. Get a car!" he ordered.

"Where?"

"You're a thief aren't you?" Derrick was thinking on his feet. "Meet me back here in ten minutes."

It didn't take Bruno ten minutes to find the right car, a nondescript eighties Toyota hatch, the typical kids joy ride, flog 'em and burn 'em type. "Where we going?" Bruno asked snapping the little car into second.

"Slow down, slow down we don't want to be noticed. Go back to our room at the apartment block." Bruno looked at Derrick he didn't question him. "They don't know us, there was a bit of a disturbance, but we've been away."

"Ok."

"I didn't book the room under my name and I paid with cash."

"Ok." Bruno agreed.

"Mr. Wagner, Mr. Wagner," the girl on reception called as Derrick Fullerton and his companion headed toward the stairs to the second floor. He didn't recognize the name. Bruno nudged him.

"Oh yes."

"We have been trying to contact you," the receptionist was quietly stressed "the phone number you left wasn't right and nor was the address."

"What!" Derrick said in feigned disbelief.

The young receptionist turned the register around for her guest to check.

"Oh that's my old address, I've done it again." He was convincing in absent minded mode. He pulled a phone from his pocket and shook his head. "I can't get used to these."

"We forgive you" the inexperienced girl was tricked by knowhow, "we needed to contact you as we had a disturbance here and I'm sorry to tell you but your room was broken into."

"What!" Derrick was very convincing with his act. He knew it was broken into before this simple little thing standing opposite him did. He also knew who did it, but he couldn't identify him.

"Was anything taken, have the Police been informed?" the dramatics continued.

"I'm so sorry Mr. Wagner," the receptionist wore all the guilt.

"The Police have investigated and we have had the locks fixed, the Police asked me to call them when you returned, I told them," the girl went on, "there were four of you staying in the room."

"The others had to leave, we just dropped them at the airport" Derrick thought he had covered everything well.

"Fine," the girl said picking up the phone, "I'll call the Police they want to talk to you."

"No, no, we'll check the room then we'll go and see them. Where is the Police Station?" Derrick had to have control.

"As you wish, go to the bottom of the street, then left up the hill."

If the girl had been a little more observant she would have seen small beads of sweat on her guest's brow and noticed how he wanted to get out of there when he grabbed the keys.

"Grab everything, find a back door to this joint and get that car of yours going." Derrick instructed as he burst through the door. He went to the robe and pulled out the third drawer, he breathed a sigh of relief. His heart rate came back substantially. His back-up gun was still there.

Down in the underground car park five minutes later Bruno struggled with a jack and the two discarded bricks to get the old Falcon high enough off the ground to get the spare wheel on. Derrick Fullerton stood alongside the mess he found himself in and pondered at the scenarios. There were twenty days left on his contract. Twenty days to deliver.

The jack slipped, the two bricks crumbled under the weight of the car and the language from Bruno was loud and foul. Derrick heard nothing, he was scared. Gunnar Hagen threatened to kill him if he came near the salvage boat again. Sandy Horder outsmarted him with his illusiveness and once reception realized he had gone, she would call the cops.

He walked towards the up ramp and looked up at this, the underside of paradise. He had the two Italians, the salvage boat, all was within his grasp. All was taken from him, taken by Sandy Horder.

Jimmy Zininski turned up at the apartment block. He mainly came to see what had happened to the old Falcon car he had rigged up on bricks and was surprised to see somebody trying to make it right. He couldn't stay away and casually walked down the ramp past Derrick Fullerton

"Having trouble there mate?"

"What's it look like?"

"It looks like tyre trouble."

"Yeah it is tyre trouble. Some smarty pinched the wheel, tyre and all."

"Some people," Jimmy was gloating.

Derrick Fullerton looked at Jimmy; he didn't like people intruding in his space.

"What do you want?"

Jimmy barred up. "Just looking,"

"I know you." Jimmy froze.

"I don't think we've met," there was nervousness in his voice.

"You were at the first Motel we stayed at. The first break in, the day we booked in you spoke to the receptionist."

He's got me, Jimmy thought.

Bruno was there in a flash and grabbed Jimmy from behind.

"You're mad I've never seen either of you before."

"You will take us to Sandy Horder," Derrick smiled. He pulled the gun from his belt. "Get this car going. Now!"

"Yes sir." The crooks were smiling they weren't beaten yet.

Jimmy was forced to help with fitting the wheel onto the car he had disabled days before. Why did he come here? Lay low were Sandy's orders.

"Get in. You're the navigator." Derrick instructed as he pushed Jimmy into the passenger seat.

"Head out, up past the cop shop," he told Bruno "We don't want to be anywhere near the law if the fellow wants to make a noise or if I have to with this," he poked the back of the seat with the gun just pass the Police Station "Which way?" Derrick yelled agitated.

"I don't know what you're talking about."

There was a muffled discharge. The muzzle of the gun was buried deep into the back of the front seat. The bullet went through the seat millimetres from Jimmy's side pocket through the firewall and ricocheted off the engine block.

"Head out to Soldiers Point,"

"Which way?"

"Right, next right."

The old Falcon followed the water around until they slowed for the small shopping strip in the fishing hamlet.

"Where now?"

"Straight up left at the top of the hill," Jimmy was giving his friends away. He vowed to fix things.

Bruno went pass the turn, Jimmy saw his chance. He undid his seat belt, lifted the door handle and threw himself out of the moving car.

Derrick Fullerton wasn't going to let another chance go, he was out and gave chase before the car stopped.

Bruno floored the old car. There was a screech of tyres and banging of doors as he pulled the wheel down to join in on the pursuit.

Jimmy gave the game away again as he headed down to the Marina.

Derrick found the speed he didn't know he had and in the last bit of desperation crash tackled Jimmy to the ground.

An old couple on their morning constitutional was astounded at the scene that befell them. "What! What is going on here?" The old man blurted out.

"We're making a movie, you either spoilt it, or you're in it." Derrick pulled Jimmy up by the collar. Bruno skidded to a halt beside them.

"What about that Dorothy?" The old lady clutched her hands under her chin speechless.

"Well what have we here?" Derrick observed several people on the Marina looking up at the to-do that had intruded their bliss. One notable was Sandy Horder who had just finished filling the *Sugar Bay* at the marine bowser.

"Park the car, then join me," Derrick ordered.

Jimmy walked awkwardly along the Marina boardwalk with Derrick's gun poking his left rib cage. There were no niceties as the pair approached Sandy who was securing the caps of the cruiser's tanks.

"Fix the man up without a word," Derrick indicated the gun to Sandy as he jabbed his hostage in the ribs, "then we're all going for a ride."

Sandy was cornered with Jimmy as the bad guy's surety.

"You will end up in trouble here," Sandy said stalling for time.

"Here comes my man," Derrick Fullerton indicated towards Bruno who was hurrying along the boardwalk after parking the car. "Let's get aboard."

Derrick pushed Bruno and Jimmy down onto the deck then summoned Sandy, who aired suspicious hesitation.

Derrick was on his game; he scanned the deck and noticed that the hatch under the bridge was not closed properly. "Get out to the open water," he instructed Sandy. In a minute the big marine diesels rumbled, there was a slight jolt and the fine craft eased away from the wharf. "Let us see what's down here," Derrick said three minutes out.

"No, don't shoot," the Italians volunteered with their hands up.

"Well, well, this is great, the boat is fuelled up and this fellow is going to tell us where to go. Get up here you two. Search down there," he ordered Bruno.

"There's storage under the seats, but it's locked," Bruno protested.

"You know how to deal with that." Derrick was in command at last as the elegant cruiser put the Marina behind them. There was a crashing of expensive timber as a number twelve boot went through the storage seat.

"Look what we got here," Bruno felt part of the old winning team as he carried out a diving tank and mask.

"Been down have we?" Derrick looked up at the bridge.

Sandy knew they were in trouble if these guys opened the other storage seat. He shut the motors down. "Look that's mine, we don't know where this so called treasure is," Sandy tried a bit of reasoning.

Derrick was on a roll. He took the gun out of Jimmy's side and pointed it up at Sandy on the bridge. "Nobody told you to stop, keep going. What else is down there?" he demanded looking back to the doorway. There was another smashing of timber then quiet. It was a long twenty seconds before Bruno dipped his head under the opening bearing the .303 and the orb.

The thieves could see their goal right here, Derrick Fullerton would fulfil his contract and he would be out of the clutches of Ivan Sandvic. "What have you got there?" The orb's value was evident in its medieval casting. Some of the gems and stones had been exposed by the boys on the *Sugar Bay* at the initial raising from the depths. The rest were shrouded by the green ugly algae now starting to harden and crack in the changed dry environment. "Where was this?"

Bruno turned to lead his boss into the forward section. "You watch them. Is that loaded?" Derrick asked.

Bruno pulled back the bolt and nodded, he was nervous, at last they were winning.

"If anybody moves," Derrick waved his hand gun around his hostages and up at Sandy, "shot 'em." He went into the forward section.

Bruno walked to the rear of the cruiser and leaned on the railing, with the sun at his back he flicked the safety on his gun and smiled the smile of a winner.

Sandy and his friends were in trouble, he couldn't take on two cheap crooks with two guns, but letting them have the treasure just wasn't an option. The phone rang in Sandy's pocket. He held up his hands as a gesture. Derrick was back in the doorway, he looked up at the bridge. "Answer it."

"Sandy, I haven't seen the little fellow this morning," Steve queried, "he was to pick me up, we were going to meet you at the Marina."

"Oh."

"Who is it?" Derrick demanded from the deck.

"Who's that, are you on the boat?" Steve wouldn't want to intrude.

"Who are you talking to?" Derrick raised his voice as he does when he can't get the answer he wants.

"It's a fishing mate," Sandy answered, letting Steve hear the conversation.

"Is that who I think it is?"

"Yes, yes you're right, I'll call you next week," Sandy feigned the conversation to throw Derrick off, and make Steve suspicious. It worked. Steve knew he had to act quickly.

"What's going on?" Maurice walked up to Steve who was sitting on a bench in front of the Country Club overlooking Shoal Bay.

"Sandy could be in trouble and if my guess is right Jimmy is with him." Both men looked out at the salvage boat moored out in the bay.

"Do you think they are on that?" Maurice pointed to the old steel hulk sitting steady on a stretched anchor line.

"I don't think so, but," Steve was thoughtful, "maybe someone from there is with them."

Just then a small white Mazda pulled up in front of the two men. Steve turned. It was Walt McEnroe and Dick Walker. "Good on you boys," Steve and Maurice rose. "I was just telling Maurice here I rang Sandy this morning and I think they're in trouble."

"Why, what did he say?" Dick who would be the least helpful in a fight had to ask.

"That's it Dick. He didn't seem free to talk."

"What? He's held against his wishes?"

"And I think Jimmy too," Steve replied looking again out into the bay.

"Well call the cops!" Dick had already wiped his hands of any altercation.

"Hey isn't that the old salvage ship?" Dick screwed his face against the water's glare.

"Yep."

"Are they on it?"

"Dunno, don't think so," Steve kept staring and thinking. "I think they are up at Soldiers Point, on Sandy's boat but they have to come past here if they want to get to the treasure."

"How do we stop them?" Dick had all the questions but no solutions.

"We'll have to get them before they leave," Steve answered "we'd better go."

"What do we do when we get there?" It was Dick's old friend Walt who now started with the questions.

None of these fellows are going to be of much help if things get bad, Steve was worried. "We'll locate the *Sugar Bay* first," Steve at least showed a level head.

"If they're in trouble we should call the cops." Dick was a fisherman and an afternoon drinker not an 'Avenger'. This justified Steve's thought.

"Keep an eye out we'll get glimpses of the water on the way." Steve assumed Sandy's position and dismissed the remark. From there on it was a quiet trip each man in his own thoughts.

In a quarter of an hour they arrived at the hill almost at the Point itself. "Drive down to the boat ramp," Steve instructed Walt who was driving. The old man was hesitant. "If some of those blokes are on the *Sugar Bay* they won't know this car."

Half way down they spotted the *Sugar Bay* motionless about half a kilometre out. Walt drove into the car park which was now almost full of empty boat trailers. "We'll walk down to the top of the ramp,' Steve said, "let Sandy know we're here."

They walked aimlessly down the hill as tourists would until they were at the top of the concrete ramp which led down into the water. "Spread out across here so Sandy can see us."

Back on the *Sugar Bay* the mood was relief. The treasure had been uncovered and secured. Derrick Fullerton would hand over the orb to Ivan Sandvic and he and Bruno would mosey back to the Gold Coast and take up where they left off with this, a successful mission under their belt.

For twenty minutes or more Derrick Fullerton couldn't leave the orb alone, he took some stainless steel cleaner Sandy kept for the railings and started cleaning it, occasionally dipping it into the water off the loading platform at the back of the boat to rinse the cleaner and show the magnificence of the gems. There was no hiding it out here out of view; he was just cleaning a centuries old precious artifact which historians would later place a value on of fifteen million dollars. He looked up, back to shore.

"Look at those four blokes standing at the top of the boat ramp," he laughed for the first time in long while; "if they could see what I have here they wouldn't believe it." Everyone looked to the shore. Derrick and Bruno were the only ones not to recognize Steve Flint, Walt McEnroe, Dick Walker and Maurice Campbell. The big four.

Sandy smiled when he saw Jimmy look over at him; he casually took the three steps to the bridge, took the phone from his pocket, pressed Steve Flints redial and put the phone on the dash over the wheel.

Steve took the phone from his pocket; he squinted trying to see the people on board the *Sugar Bay* . Voices could be heard which prompted Steve to press the speaker button.

"Well this is what we came for Mr. Smarty," Derrick said while fondly caressing the orb.

"And how are you going to get away with it?" Sandy carefully encouraged the conversation.

"I'd say, we'll take your friend here with us as insurance," Derrick indicated to Jimmy, "after all he led us to you."

"I'm sorry Sandy."

"Don't worry about it Jimmy, we'll be right."

The boys on shore listened intently as the conversation went on.

"I don't see how you'll be right." Derrick turned angry, "we've got the guns and the loot."

On shore Dick Walker grabbed Steve Flint's arm, he was watching a thriller movie.

Back on the boat Bruno stepped down into the forward section and rustled about in the second storage cabinet. He found the small black bags.

"What is it?" Derrick was coming down in confidence and up in irritability at Sandy's 'we'll be right' remark when

Bruno stepped through the hatch onto the deck clutching two black bags.

Realizing immediately the impact the diamonds would have Sandy bent down over the phone. "Wave like hell," it was a loud whisper.

Bruno showed the open bag to a surprised Derrick Fullerton.

"What!"

"What's happening on shore?" Sandy shouted to a confused group on deck.

Jimmy went along. "They're trying to tell us something!" he yelled.

Derrick looked to shore, then back to the diamonds.

They all got in on the act, "Fire!" Muscat Farincini bellowed and pointed to shore throwing the crooks attention again. There was three point four two eight seconds to act. Here comes the cavalry.

Sandy twisted the key, engaged drive and pulled the go levers right the way back. Just inside the allotted time. The others read the scene perfectly and grabbed something to steady themselves two hundredth of a second before the drive was engaged. Breaking things down further, on propeller water impact, Derrick Fullerton dropped the orb and lost his footing, then with a little help from Jimmy did a rather awkward water entry off the rear of the cruiser. Bruno was surprised not only by the powerful forward thrust of the Captain's actions but by Muscat's hairy left elbow going right into his mouth. The orb was relinquished on the deck of the *Sugar Bay* and the wind, along with some teeth and blood, were knocked out of him as Muscat shoulder charged him over the railing of the *Sugar Bay* .

"Good work boys, throw them a rope Jimmy." Sandy smiled as he turned the cruiser to circle the two water fowl. "We'll tow them in closer to shore," and then he picked up the phone, "Steve meet us at The Anchorage."

Half an hour later the treasure and crew were reunited at the wharf of the Anchorage Resort. "We've had a bit of a mishap," Sandy told the boys on the back of the *Sugar Bay*, "and it's going to be hard to get out of the heads with all eyes watching us, I suggest we lay low for a week."

"Are we going back for the rest of the treasure?" Maurice asked.

"Oh yeah," Sandy was sure about that.

"Good."

"I'll take our two friends here up and around to the Myall Lakes for a week and stay out of sight, the rest of you are ok except for Jimmy," he hesitated, "they know Jimmy."

Sandy looked at the youngest member of the crew, "You had better take your wife for a holiday."

"Yep."

"I don't expect the salvage boat to hang around long," Sandy explained, "somebody's got to be paying them, and it wouldn't be cheap."

"Will we split up now?" Dick asked.

"Yes you can keep in touch by phone; otherwise we meet back here in a week."

The men filed off except for the two Italians.

It was Sandy's plan to stay away further up in the reaches of Port Stephens for about a week. Firstly to get the *Sugar Bay* out of sight, thus keep the crooks guessing, and secondly to try and starve them out. They just can't sit around waiting for the next move.

Jimmy looked at the old dilapidated building site, a left over remnant from the last building boom. It had a great hill position over-looking the fishing co-operative and the beautiful Bay. But when the boom is over, the speculators go home, the developer goes broke and the once gambled vision is left a steel and timber carcass to be devoured by the elements.

It wasn't the only idle project at the Bay, but it suited this sometime fisherman turned treasure hunter. It was quiet and out of the way and it had just what he was looking for. It wasn't hard to shift two panels of the construction fence and by doing so the little polish migrant knew he had broken the law.

"I'll bring it back" he looked to where we all believe heaven is.

As Jimmy backed his trailer through the opening and up to the builders cage he had spotted earlier he prepared to break the next law. Getting the cumbersome six foot steel mesh cube onto the trailer was done in a blind panic as was the exit from the site which left some of his car's paint and the left guard of the trailer on the partially opened construction fence.

Jimmy Zininiski devised the safety cage when he saw builders using an electrically operated version, using chains, pulleys and an electric motor. Jimmy utilized an engine lifter by extending the arm with the block and tackle on the lift and equally extending a bar as an anchor on the opposite side. The whole thing would then have to be secured to the deck of the *Sugar Bay* .

"What do you think?" Jimmy asked when he showed his handiwork to Steve Flint, the man who would use it.

"Nothing will get into that."

"I've welded in extra one inch round bar on every side it helps to keep it rigid" Jimmy went on, "and the lock, just pull the door and this spring loaded clasp fastens onto the frame."

"You've done a great job Jimmy, this will keep me safe and we can lift up whatever else I find down there. That block and tackle is designed to lift an engine out of a car, with the help of water weightlessness this thing," he pointed to the pulleys on the boom, "could probably pull the old wreck from the sea bed."

"Well anything we want to bring up." Jimmy admired his own work.

CHAPTER 23

ENTER ATHOL D'LARGE

Meanwhile on the other side of the country, investigations are being made into unsolved crimes. The floundering conservative party needed to get some runs on the board in social justice. A contract was issued to the high profile Prosecutor Athol D'Large from the east coast. He came to Perth in Western Australia also with a letter of introduction to the Perth Wildcats 'A' league soccer team. At twenty five he had two successful years playing 'A' league on the east coast as well as a degree in criminal law and a post graduate degree in forensic science. He had done the D'Large family name well by excelling in both law and football, a trait his grandfather, the original Athol D'Large initiated and nurtured in the generations that followed him.

Football was a natural, if you have the gene and if it is cultivated you have the edge. Add discipline to the mix and you can become a champion. Athol D'Large had it all and he loved the game. The same brilliant mind that kept him in front of the ball on the pitch kept the same man in front of the game in the courtroom. The perfect example being The State verses Bobby King.

"I put it to you Mr. King you were in The Royal Oak on Thursday the twenty seventh."

"I was not. I was at me girlfriend's house."

"She said you left at ten."

"That's right, so how could I be at the pub at ten fifteen?"

There was quiet, the defendant smiled at his girlfriend in the Courtroom. The Judge looked questioningly at the Prosecutor.

The Prosecutor caught the link between the defendant and his girlfriend. He looked at Bobby King then at the girlfriend.

"Is that your girlfriend in the third row?"

"Objection!"

"Yeah that's right."

"Your Honour I object, the prosecution can't choose people out of the gallery."

"Over ruled."

"Well who was the girl you had in the pub that night?"

"You rat Bobby King."

"Your Honour I object, my client…"

Athol D'Large sat down. His assistant leaned over.

"How did you know that?"

"I was saving it. Rather dramatic don't you think?"

****

"ÝES, I SAW HIM on the news the other night," Detective Inspector Ray McCormick didn't look up from his desk in his office in an inner suburban Perth Police Station when he was asked by a subordinate of the impending stint by this hot shot from the east at their Baker Street precinct.

"What's he going to do?"

"We might make him Captain of the football team" the senior man said as he pressed 'save' on his keyboard, pushed his chair away from the desk and looked at the younger man standing in the doorway.

"We don't have a football team."

The joke was dead. Senior Constable Michael Davies, Acting Assistant Prosecutor could see his career slipping into the doldrums. Here was a man almost forty, still only three years into an eight year part time law degree, the cushiest job at the station, now looking at mundane police duties encompassing shift work.

"Well Senior Constable we will have to see what the powers that be intend for him."

Ray McCormick was a fair man, as long as the police under his charge did the right thing in a difficult situation he stood by them.

"This bloke has two law degrees. He'll out qualify our Prosecutor." Michael said feeling a bit short at this point.

"And me." Ray agreed.

"With all due respects Sir, you do have the position."

"We will wait and see what happens Senior Constable." Ray stood up. The conversation was over.

On Monday morning a television cameraman and interviewer, the local radio newsman and the reporter from the West Australian were on hand to report the arrival and initiation of Athol D'Large as the Primary Investigative Case Administrator to work out of Baker Street precinct.

The State Commissioner introduced Mr. D'Large to the press in a speech written and rehearsed at the end of the previous week.

"We poached Mr. D'Large from under the noses of the east coast governments and the powerful law firms, not to play football, (pause for laughs from gathered crowd) but to initiate and conduct a more investigative appraisal of some of our current cases."

What this all meant was that the Premier had been onto the Commissioner about the lack of closure on so many outstanding criminal cases in recent years.

"I want to see the Selby Securities case solved with publicity," the Commissioner was told, "and another headliner on the front page."

"Resources Sir, we don't have them."

"Get them, I want to see something in the papers in weeks, we have an election in seven months!"

Athol D'Large was headlines on the back page of the national papers for his football prowess. The family name and the successful Prosecutor were always linked. This was a unique package and real coup for the Western Australian Government.

"Football star solves cases." Was the headline that was going to get the conservative government over the line for a record breaking fourth term.

The Commissioner got the country's top Prosecutor's name on the contract; he was going to be there every inch of the way.

"Well there you have it Senior Constable Davies," the Detective Inspector assured his underling, "you keep your job, but you should try to finish that degree, smart blokes like Athol D'Large are coming and they'll take over. Besides that," the senior went on, "a degree will give you a pay rise, and that makes for a bigger pension in the end."

"Where will he sit?"

"We'll have to give him your office."

"And where..?"

"Hey," the Detective Inspector was fair, "you'll work it out."

Athol D'Large was distinguished. He wore well cut dark suits, two tone shirts and wore trademark bright patterned ties. On his first day on the job Detective Inspector McCormick gathered the Police and the administration staff in his office for their introduction.

"Thank you Detective Inspector, as you have been made aware my sole purpose for being here in your Police Station is to have a base for my work as Primary Investigative Case Administrator, not to interfere with cases you are working on, but to get closure on and look differently at other aspects of other cases not only in your Precinct but elsewhere." He tried to put everyone at ease. "Your jobs are safe, I am independent, I appreciate Senior Constable Davies giving up his office, and I hope I'm not too much of an inconvenience."

"That's fine," the Senior Constable waved from the back of the room. They loved him he was the genuine product.

"What about the football?"

"No football this year." Athol D'Large looked at the office clerk who was resting on the chief's desk.

"I have an eighteen month contract, I have to deliver. I may not even see a game," he smiled.

"Well that's going to shoot my little bloke down," one of the Highway Patrol Officers threw in.

"We may try to get him to a game," he won them over completely. "Thanks everyone I must get to work." He nodded and made his way sideways to the door.

"Not a bad bloke."

"Yeah."

"Different to the way he appears."

"Like the man said," the Detective Inspector indicated the meeting was over.

There weren't boxes of files moved in the big change over just a laptop. All contact with whoever he dealt with was done on a mobile phone. It seemed the laptop and the phone went with Athol D'Large everywhere.

His door was always closed but he greeted everybody equally after the civil knock, one of the first such inquires was from the former inhabitant of the office. "Is everything ok? Is there anything I can get you?" The Senior Constable just wanted to make contact. Part of working in a small station like Baker Street is being on the team. Workwise everybody knew what their area was like. Everybody shared information.

Socially they had their drinking haunt, a small older style beer garden at the back of Mrs. Fowler's Club House Hotel, otherwise known as The Chicken House. The cops drank there, most locals stayed away. "Thanks, everything is fine at the moment," Athol closed his laptop and gestured to the chair opposite.

"So you're looking at the Selby Securities fraud?"

"Yes," the new man answered, "it's no secret," he didn't elaborate.

"Do you know who did it?"

"Yes."

"You're joking?" The Senior Constable was getting too friendly, as was his way.

"No, I'll nail them both."

"Both!"

"Keep this quiet for a couple of weeks the Commissioner wants front page arrests. Tell me," Athol went on, "what are you working on?"

"The usual drink drive, domestic violence. District Court as you know gets a bit messy," he replied as he looked at the man opposite him. "Do you like your job?"

"Oh yeah. Do you like yours?"

"There's no glamour in small time drugs busts and drunken pub brawls."

"Davies there is no glamour in crime."

"Yes but," the Senior Constable tried to point out, "these people you chase will be the champions of the press when they're caught. The scum we prosecute are led into Court with an old jumper over their heads, names suppressed to protect the innocent."

"We all go for a conviction, and we all have our disappointments, mine is watching two guys being led away for four years after fraudulently stealing a couple of million dollars.

"People don't see it that way. The money came from an institution no loses."

"No. The race course principle applies. Bookie - punter. Someone always wins, someone always loses." Athol said.

"Ok, I don't mean to intrude on your time." The Senior Constable got up.

"You come in any time," Athol opened his laptop.

"Thanks, if you're on for a beer, we meet most afternoons at the Chicken House."

"Pardon me?"

"Oh, the local pub."

"Chicken House, catchy name."

"Our name," the Senior Constable explained. "The Publican is Mrs. Fowler. Fowls, chooks, chickens."

"Got it, mum's the word on Selby Securities." Michael Davies nodded. It was the good ice breaker.

Athol D'Large never met with people other than the police staff in his office at Baker Street Police Station. Being high profile as he was, it was not unusual for him to leave around lunch time and not be seen until the next morning. It was also not unusual for him to be quoted in the newspaper or to hold a joint press conference with the Commissioner or the department head. He was Baker Street's mystery man. He was bigger than Baker Street.

CHAPTER 24

THE INVESTIGATOR

Kevin Tucker and Athol D'Large had been friends since school days. Both bright scholars they graduated from Sydney University Athol in Law, Kevin in Economics. Kevin soon went down the IT path. He was the investigator. Back on the East Coast on the soccer pitch Athol and Kevin knew each other's game they each knew what the other was thinking. The dribble, the short pass, the dribble, the long pass. Athol was always there. Near the goal, it was split second panic.

"Don't split them up," every Club Manager said, "they're a team."

Eventually the split came, not through football contracts, through their professional careers. Athol had kept his career and his spot on the A League Team until this contract came up in Perth. He knew this was the next step. Kevin kept his spot on the A League Team and helped Athol using his computer skills. Athol built the case, Kevin was the spy.

In his third week in the west Athol met with his friend in an inner suburban Perth pub.

"Kevin, good to see you."

"You too, how's it going?"

"You tell me."

"I've got them." Kevin slapped his old friend on the back.

"You're kidding? Great. Another case closed, I'm shouting."

When the lawyer came back to the table, Kevin elaborated.

"Yep, two million dollars went into G.W.S minerals on twenty third July last year, it was a long shot, and they must have had information because it paid off. They got out the next morning."

"How could they be so blatant?"

"I'd say they got the information and acted on it straight away. Just took the money out of the till."

Athol looked at his friend and breathed in deep. "You've got the hard copy of this?"

"And I've got the copies of the broker's buy and sell contracts."

Kevin Tucker flew over from Sydney especially for this informal meeting. "When are you coming back Athol?"

"I have an eighteen month contract."

"Well you have been here three weeks and you solved the first big one in the West."

"You solved it."

"No you found the crook, I found the emails, look buy out the contract. You can make more money playing football than catching crooks."

Athol laughed. Another case solved thanks to Kevin Tucker.

"When are you going back?" Athol asked his friend.

"Training tomorrow afternoon."

"Ok I'll tidy this up and give it to the Commissioner on Thursday."

"What else have you got?"

"There are a few in here," Athol picked up the laptop and smiled, "they're pretty straight forward."

"Fraudster purchases luxury unit on beach and buys Maserati," his friend pointed out the flaws of the nouveau riche.

"Yes not too hard to track down,' Athol agreed.

"And the old gentry go unnoticed." Kevin Tucker was alluding to the fact that two privileged public school boys with gleaming ancestry could use hacking skills and family contacts to catch these classless knaves.

"I don't know," Athol shook his head.

"What?"

"There's a bloke in here," Athol tapped the top of his laptop; "I could take the Assistant Prosecutor around to his office tomorrow and arrest him."

"Why don't you?"

"Why don't they, the cops?"

"You tell me."

"They don't have the hard evidence."

"And you?"

"There's a new Cooper S and a Ducati Super Sport at his new unit, oh and he just left his wife."

"How do you know this?"

"I made one phone call to his wife, she told me about the unit, and I drove past and spotted the new toys."

"Oh."

"I haven't brought you into this one yet, they haven't given it to me. If they do you will find both toys are on a minimum commercial lease with little or no residual. The man is washing money through the leases." There was a forced smile.

"Why don't they give it to you?"

"Probably not big enough."

"Oh."

"Headlines mate. The Premier wants headlines."

"You're getting sick of it, I can tell."

"No, no, I want a big one," he touched the laptop again, "there are no big ones in here,"

"Well work with the cops on the Cooper S and the Ducati."

"They don't want to, they want to sit in the pub and talk about cops and robbers. Or sit in their office and talk about cops and robbers. They don't do what you do."

Kevin Tucker turned his head and squinted.

"Privacy laws," Athol pursed his lips. "You've got to watch those privacy laws."

"They may catch themselves in their privates." There followed raucous laughter.

Three days later a foreign exchange trader and the company secretary were marched out of the Selby Securities building in handcuffs and onto the big screens of every living room in Western Australia. The Premier's press conference was played every half hour on the twenty four hour news channel.

Another case closed.

CHAPTER 25

ANOTHER LOOK AT THE BANK NOTE
REFUBISHMENT CASE

There was the familiar knock on Athol's office door. Senior Constable Michael Davies held the morning paper.

"You got 'em, you said you would and you said there were two!" he was excited for Athol D'Large. Anything that happened in the Baker Street Precinct was a team effort, whether it is an arrest or a conviction, and it took time to conclude.

This was a one man show. Senior Constable Davies didn't know about Kevin Tucker. In three weeks this one man wonder had another arrest.

"That's incredible, they heaped praise on you and to quote," Michael looked down at the paper, 'your quick closure.'"

"Yes I read it at breakfast, he's a good man your Premier."

"Will you be Prosecuting?"

"No, the Crown will appoint a silk, maybe I'll assist," Athol allowed a slight grin, "take on your role."

"But why not you?" The Senior Constable defended.

"Takes too much time. There are other crooks to catch." Athol played down his role. "I handed over my work to the District Attorney's Office yesterday afternoon."

"What!"

Athol D'Large looked without saying a word at the astonished Senior Constable. "I've seen a truck load of files, a team of four and nine months work out there," he pointed to somewhere beyond the adjoining wall, "to investigate a suspicious factory fire," he hesitated "with no conviction."

"We haven't got a conviction yet." Athol played it down yet again.

"They should have had you on the Bank Note Refurbishment case."

"The what?"

"The big bank note change over job a while back." The Senior Constable opened an old file in the memory side of his brain.

"Don't know it." Athol D'Large said.

"What was his name?" the Senior Constable squinted and twisted his mouth. "Johnson, Johnno Johnson."

"Doesn't ring any bells," Athol was still none the wiser.

"He was running some kind of foreign exchange manipulative inside the bank note refurbishment centre."

"That sounds interesting."

Senior Constable Michael Davies felt some importance. "It was a big deal, ten million bucks!" The Senior Constable played all of his cards.

Two days later Athol D'Large had several pages of research on his laptop pertaining to The Banknote Refurbishment case. He went through each transaction and saw the pattern. Wait until the deal was set and signed, and then pick the highest point of the targeted currency. Do the conversion of half the capital into the lowest currency valued at that time, as soon as the targeted currency moves up, helped by this false transaction, buy in with the other half of the capital. Manipulation at its finest. No greed, just a game. A fixed game. Where is the money? It's not missing. There were bank note refurbishment transactions. It was bought in as old stock and sold out for disposure. All computer entered. Everything balanced.

Most international deals are done in US dollars, it being the standard for gold, oil and the highly traded commodities. The buyers in these cases will sometimes use currencies other than US dollars. They could use gold in the lead up and switch once a point is gained. Points and parts of points in a half a billion dollar deal is a lot of yen, rand, or whatever the home currency could be.

Daily Clearance was the case. Johnno Johnson was the culprit. How did he convert the skimmings that he took off the top of international transactions into transportable cash? Athol D'Large went through the transaction reports and the country of origin surveys several times looking for something, anything.

Transactions could be done in US dollars, currency of choice or gold, or a combination. When the purchaser was satisfied with the deal, it was set in place. The Department then did the conversation into Australian dollars.

Athol D'Large got this. It was straight forward.

He went over it again and again until he saw the time stream. Two days, sometimes three days before the monies were transferred into the seller bank account. Why? Because Johnno Johnson held it up.

This fellow Johnno Johnson wasn't a genius he just took risks with other people's money, swapping currencies in his favour in those extra days, then transferring the funds into the relevant company's accounts and walking away. When it was all done he simply bought gold with his takings sold it back for currency and took the haul out of the establishment in untraceable old notes destined for disposal.

Because no one lost money the federal investigators didn't make a case. And because of that, they didn't see how the money was taken out of the building, and they wouldn't have even been called in if the new stand in Manager hadn't discovered that the last transaction Johnno Johnson dealt with was in fact in credit.

There were fourteen transactions. It totalled ten million dollars. There was no money missing. There was an embarrassing amount of money left over. This was a big deal and everyone missed it.

Athol D'Large could see The Daily Clearance Case as his premiership. Big fish like this don't come along often, and big ones wrapped in intrigue never come along. He set up meetings with the department of treasury head also the Manager Daily Clearance and Bank Note Refurbishment and allowed himself three days to assess his findings.

Carl Betz was back in his old job as Manager of Domestic Business when he got the call from Athol D'Large to set up a meeting.

"How can I help Mr. D'Large?" he said into the mouthpiece as he leaned back in his three way adjustable chair.

"I was hoping you could find the time to talk to me about the Daily Clearance Case."

"I'm not there anymore. That was only a temporary transfer."

"I know. I'd like to talk to you about Mr. John Thomas Johnson."

"Sure, did you say you were with the Attorney General's Department?"

"That's right, can we make a time to meet."

"Yes I can make time tomorrow, what's this about?"

"It's about the money Mr. Betz."

Carl Betz held the phone away from his ear and looked at it. He thought this day would come, although he knew nothing of the fraud, he was in charge of the unit. The subsequent investigation, which turned up nothing, took place under his watch. "What money?"

"Tomorrow afternoon two o'clock suit you?" The sleuth asked.

"Yes, see you then."

Carl Betz was impressed when he greeted the very well dressed younger man in his office the next day. "Pleased to meet you Mr. D'Large. When you rang to arrange this appointment I didn't realize that you were the investigator who solved the Selby Securities case."

"We got lucky." Athol smiled and looked around.

"Please." Carl Betz withdrew his hand and gestured to a comfortable armed chair. He moved around the desk and eased himself into his three way adjustable chair. As not a lot happens in the position Manager Domestic Business, Carl

Betz was happy to cancel all meetings formal and informal for the day. To meet with someone other than a department colleague was indeed unusual. He took the liberty of ordering beverage.

"Can I offer you tea or coffee that's as strong as it gets around here."

Athol D'Large laughed politely. "Tea will be just right thank you."

Carl Betz picked up the phone it was all prearranged. Break out the good cups and buy a packet of biscuits. "Could you bring in two cups of your finest please," the smile was part of the act.

Carl Betz eased back in his chair as he does; he was never comfortable in the company of strangers for the first time. It's not uncommon in government departments. Personnel in most positions like Carl Betz went into the public service initially because it was not unlike school, you sat for and passed grade exams and went to the next level. Mothers liked the public service because it offered security. So consequently the same people were thrown in with the same people who didn't have a lot of contact outside the department. They were wary of personnel from other departments and considered private enterprise the pits of unknown and of no virtue.

The Manager of Domestic Business looked down at his fingers, and told himself to start a conversation that would interest the other person who was sitting quietly watching the nervousness. "That case of Selby Securities made the headlines, how did you get onto them?"

Athol D'Large stared straight at Carl. He knew he was only a caretaker manager after the event but department managers should be leaned on, for three hundred and sixty four days a year Carl Betz was a tea and bickies man. Today he would account for the time he spent sitting in John Thomas Johnson's chair. "Well Mr. Betz it comes down to who has access, then you follow a spending trail."

"They all do the same thing I suppose." Carl Betz eased himself into his three way adjustable chair.

"Pretty much," the investigator answered keeping the investigative face. "If you just outsmarted someone out of a million dollars you may as well buy a flash car and show everyone."

"Well that's not the case with this one." Carl Betz went straight into what they were here to talk about, he leaned forward. "There's no money."

"Yes Mr. Betz there is."

"Has everyone missed something?"

"You tell me, in the Department of Treasury as acting Manager of Daily Clearance and bank note rejuvenation you oversaw the investigation of missing departmental funds."

The tea and bickies came in. Carl looked at his assistant with the tray. "Thank you." This now very nervous unsure of himself man thought this was going to be pleasant afternoon tea. Inside three minutes he was a drowning man gasping out of his depth.

The professional didn't move in his chair as the assistant poured tea and offered milk from stainless steel utensil scavenged for the moment. He took his eyes momentarily from the accused and nodded a yes.

"I, I don't get your meaning." Carl stumbles his words as he helped himself to the sugar and dismissed his assistant with another thank you. "No money has been found."

"But Mr. Betz," the informed prosecutor sipped from his cup "money has found to be missing."

"Where? How?" let him prove it, was the novice thought.

"Through currency trading" it was just proven without raising a threat.

"Currency trading, I know nothing about currency trading."

"You should, you were head of Daily Clearance."

It was too late to get another grip everything was slipping away from Carl Betz. Occasionally departments and department heads are called to account. Occasionally.

Mostly the Carl Betz of the system did their grade assessments and achieved the top levels, sometimes doing a part time degree. This is where serious qualifications add to the salary pack. When qualifications are assessed, which is then based on salary, various attained levels will then qualify for an acting position, as was the case when Carl Betz acted as Manager of Daily Clearance and Bank Note Rejuvenation. Carl Betz was in trouble it showed on his reddening face. He did nothing wrong.

"I was given the acting job after this so called crime was committed."

"That's when the investigation started." The star prosecutor sipped again from his tea cup.

"I went into that position because the appointed Manager passed away." Carl Betz tried to salvage some respect using Johnno Johnson's sad passing and showing himself to be doing the right thing at a very difficult time.

"That's right." Athol agreed. "If he hadn't passed away I would be having this conversation with him and I would ask him where the money was. However you were sitting in his chair immediately after his death."

"I'm no longer associated with those two departments," Carl Betz explained. "I believe two Managers have been appointed now, probably so that same situation won't happen again." He felt good. "Have you spoken to them?"

"That's not my concern," was the right way of saying, 'don't tell me how to do my job'. "There have been inter departmental changes in the aftermath of this catastrophe, however,' the prosecutor elaborated, "you took over at that time. It was your position and with position comes responsibility."

Carl Betz wasn't ready for this meeting. The word responsibility could be substituted for accountability and public service is not accountable.

"Thank you for your time Mr. Betz," Athol finished his tea "I'll be going now, you will be notified."

This was not an official investigation. It wasn't sanctioned by the Commissioner; it wasn't anything to do with Athol D'Large's contract. The man was intrigued by the uniqueness the boldness and the downright scale of the whole heist, and he was going to work it out. Carl Betz wouldn't be notified. Athol D'Large didn't like Department Managers who swanned back in their office towers and this man wasn't the first one he had left hanging.

Back in his office in Baker Street Athol D'Large mused at his computer screen. He tapped his fingers, looked at his door, and then made the decision. He got up walked out of the office and up to Detective Inspector Ray McCormick's office. He knocked lightly on the open door. "Do you have a minute Sir?"

"Of course," the senior man looked up and pointed to a chair. "How are things down in your part of the building?" Ray made a casual reference to the fact that Athol was very much a sole operator with the Commissioner's grace.

"Everything is fine, I have finished the case I was working on and handed my findings on. Ah." he hesitated "I'm delving into the Daily Clearance Case, may be get some information to hand on to the Commissioner with a view to reopening it.

"It was a puzzle that one," Detective Inspector looked at Athol warily, "it was hard to fathom if I remember correctly. There were lots of transactions but no money."

"No Detective Inspector, there was a great deal of money."

"Oh, it's a bit hazy. The main suspect died didn't he?" Ray made strange facial expressions as he dug into this file back there in his brain.

"He did, heart attack, hence the old saying, 'he took it to the grave with him.'"

"What are you going to do, dig him up?" Ray allowed himself a chuckle.

"Someone's got the money." Athol looked questioningly at Ray.

"Ok." It was serious. "What now?" asked Ray.

"Can you spare Senior Constable Davies for a day or two?"

"Of course, if we can help, what's your plan?"

"I'd like to go through everything that's out there. Find people to interview who would have been overlooked and I only have a few days, the Commissioner wants to see me next Monday."

"You can start now."

"I do appreciate this, Detective Inspector."

That afternoon, working together, Senior Constable Michael Davies and Athol D'Large had only come up with the names of the two Federal Police Officers who had investigated the case and the relevant dates. "Ring these two fellows. Just give them your name and rank and set up a meeting for me." Athol told Michael. "Let them think there's a big investigation going on."

The next morning the star sleuth was introduced to Detective George Hennesy the Chief Investigator on the Daily Clearance Case. "Mr. D'Large, it's a pleasure to meet you, so you want to open the Daily Clearance Case again?"

"Yes, it hit a curious cord."

"It certainly does that, I'll show you what we had, maybe you can figure out what Mr. Johnson did with the money. If there was any."

"You don't think there was any money?"

"No."

"What is your opinion based on?"

"The man lived the public servant's lifestyle in the suburbs. I think his widow is still living there. I mean," The federal policeman went on, "nothing came out until he died. That's when they found one transaction he was working on was in credit for two hundred thousand dollars."

"Where did this figure of ten million come from?" Athol knew it wasn't that simple.

"An investigative reporter from The West Australian."

"What was his source?"

"He had a contact inside the Department. There were a lot of rumours around, there always is with fraud."

"Did you meet with this man?"

"A couple of times, I showed him our findings which were all the transactions going back to when Mr. Johnson started at Daily Clearance, it turned out he had access to the same material."

"What are you telling me?"

"We were both reading from the same book. I didn't come up with ten million dollars, he did. I think it sold a few papers that day," the Federal Policeman added.

"You don't mind giving me your findings?" Athol asked he was literally starting where the feds left off.

"No, like I said we were open with the reporter from the West Australian as far as we're concerned it's closed. There was no money."

"What do you think?" Athol asked George Hennesy the man who spent several months investigating the case.

"There were fourteen cases where currencies were exchanged, then changed back to their currency of origin. We don't know why, the man responsible died on us. The last transaction, the Ruble was changed to the US dollar and was thus two hundred thousand dollars in credit on settlement day."

"Why was that?"

"Because it wasn't changed back to its currency of origin."

"And in the other thirteen cases the currency was changed back in the closing hours of settlement?"

"Yes."

"And the sums were done on the difference of the currency exchange and this added up to ten million or something like that?"

"Right, look I'll show you the one before that," the federal policeman had prepared some workings earlier. He rolled the mouse and clicked on transactions, it was an Indian Iron Ore deal. "See here, he goes out of the rupee to US dollars for the deal, and then switches to the British pound. The sheer weight of the transaction moves it, currency traders move in up she goes again. Our man pulls out. Look at that paper shuffle two hundred and ten thousand dollars Australian."

"Where's the money?'

"What money it was a paper shuffle."

That afternoon Athol D'Large went through every transaction done during Johnno Johnson's tenure at the Daily Clearance and Bank Note Rejuvenation. He had an exact figure of ten million six hundred thousand dollars. There wasn't a particular pattern, there wasn't a preferred currency. It was a bet, but it was a fixed bet. The amount of money transferred to a particular currency made for a movement, this attracted the vultures and as the federal policeman said 'up she goes.'

It wasn't Johnno Johnson's money and he stacked the deck. But, where was the loser here? No doubt currency traders were watching his plays, it always happened after an Australian trade deal, they jumped in and helped push everything north. Then they all got out together.

"There was serious money made here," Athol told the screen that had him engrossed. "Why would he do it if he couldn't get it out?"

The financial world wasn't going to offer assistance, this was their business. Johnno Johnson could have been watched from afar as currency traders looked for the upside edge on a contract. "If this was global his ten million was piddling." Athol rested his elbows on the desk and rubbed his forehead.

There was a tap on the door. "Come in."

It was Senior Constable Davies. "You got an early start."

"Yes I keep going over the same stuff."

"How did you get along with the Feds?"

"Good, George Hennesy, nice bloke, gave me what he had but we already had it, Public Record."

"Newspapers," The Senior Constable knew it was wrong when he said it.

"Same thing, they just dramatize theirs to sell papers.

"The stock exchange," Michael Davies looked at the man behind the computer.

"Could you imagine flashing a badge in there? They'd all fly out the windows."

Both men laughed loud. It was what they needed. "What about his wife?"

"What about the wife?"

The appointment was made for two o'clock the following afternoon. It was Friday; Athol was to meet the Commissioner the next Monday morning to be briefed on another big profile public case. If Athol couldn't come up with some positive findings to sure up his interpretation of what went on in the Daily Clearance Case by then, all would be lost.

CHAPTER 26

A VISIT TO MRS. JOHNSON

Senior Constable Michael Davies and Athol D'Large pressed the doorbell on the comfortable brick suburban home. A small neat early sixties lady with grey hair was expecting them. The Senior Constable from Baker Street did the introductions. Both men followed the well-groomed lady into her living room. The heavy drapes had been parted on a bay window. A three piece tapestry lounge, a cedar chiffonier and matching coffee table were placed well on a dark green woven carpet. "Can I offer you gentlemen tea? I usually have one myself at this time of the day." She was an educated elegant lady of style.

"Thank you Mrs. Johnson." Athol D'Large answered for them both.

The organized hostess was back before the two men had seated. "If the coffee table could be moved," Mrs. Johnson held the silver tray, "I'll pour and leave you men to do your sugar and milk."

"Thank you."

"Thank you."

"I don't have sweet biscuits, but I can recommend those savoury pieces," the lady nodded to the tray. "I get them from Aldi."

"Thank you."

"Thank you."

Athol smiled with his second 'thank you' and noted again the positive attributes of this lady. She had a comfortable life and it suited her comfortably.

"Mr. D'Large what a beautiful name I'm sure it can be traced back to an age of strong men."

"I'm not sure of the men who bore our name, but it is usually defined at length and broken down to particles at weddings and christenings."

"Mr. Davies yours is a lovely name as well," the lady wasn't leaving anyone out.

"No, no we're not royalty."

"Mrs. Johnson it's very kind of you to meet with us, the Senior Constable told you over the phone what we wanted to talk to you about…. I don't want to be traumatic." Athol knew if there was anything here this lady could tell him.

"That's fine Mr. D'Large you have a job to do," Mrs. Johnson summed these two up as well and thought they may be the ones who could bring things to a conclusion.

"Mrs. Johnson is there anything your husband did in his last couple of months that was out of character?"

"As I told the other policemen at the time, he did keep odd hours."

"How odd?"

"Ten O'clock was late for John, except for the night he died, it was after midnight I was worried sick. I knew it was something bad."

"I'm very sorry to have you go through this Mrs. Johnson."

"Yes, the doctor came to see me, he said John must have had a big shock, you see he was our family doctor and John had no ailments, but that night he had a massive heart attack while driving the car."

"He hadn't been treating your husband for anything?"

"Nothing at all. It was such a shock he was just sixty."

The Senior Constable was taking notes.

"Do you know when the heart attack occurred?"

"It was around ten o'clock, up on Bayswater Road, as I said it was midnight when they came here."

"Bayswater Road is that the road out of the city where your husband worked?"

"No."

"So he must have been somewhere after work?"

"Yes."

"Was the incident far from here, I mean this house?"

"No, only ten minutes away, poor John was almost home when he got this terrible shock."

"So they took him to hospital tried to revive him, then came to see you."

Athol D'Large put his cup down, there was nothing here, why mention the money.

"I'm sorry to put you through this again Mrs. Johnson. It has been a pleasure meeting you."

Senior Constable Michael Davies put his cup on the low table.

"Was it a bad accident Mrs. Johnson?" he asked.

"There was no accident."

"Wasn't the car damaged?"

"No John had the sense to turn off that busy road when he knew something was wrong."

"Where's the car now?" Senior Constable Davies knew that the car was the only link they had. "I sold it, you see I don't drive."

The dying flame flickered.

"Do you recall who you sold it to?" the Senior Constable prodded.

"Oh yes John and I always kept records."

It was the oxygen the flame needed. The Senior Constable retrieved his notebook. Both men sat on the lounge in silence. This was the critical part of the interview. The stylish organized hostess returned with the registration renewal certificate.

"There are his particulars, Emit Horsley."

The Senior Constable transferred the details to his notepad.

In the short time Athol D'Large spent with the Senior Constable in the company of Mrs. Johnson he could see a good person. On entering the room initially he had noted the professional standard photos of a seemingly devoted couple taken in various times of their life. "Did you have any children Mrs. Johnson?"

"No there was just John and I."

"I am sorry for your loss." It was a sincere condolence. Athol took the lady's hand. She acknowledged with a sad smile.

As the car pulled away from the curb Athol D'Large waved to the lonely lady standing at the front door. "There's nothing there."

"You're right." Michael agreed. "Let's go see Emit Horsley."

After two stops to refer to the Gregory's Street directory, the two law men found 26 Bulwer Street about forty minutes from the Johnson house.

Athol stood back and observed the surroundings as the Policeman again rang the door-bell; he knew there would be no cedar chiffonier in this sitting room.

Again a lady in her early sixties answered the door. Although she wasn't expecting them the contrast to Mrs. Johnson was of the opposite. She wore a grey track suit and slippers and touched her unkempt hair as if that would excuse her frayed look. "Yes."

"Mrs. Horsley?" Senior Constable Davies asked.

"Yes," the woman pulled the zip on her top.

"We wondered if we could speak with Mr. Horsley."

The woman looked at the Senior Constable then at the well-dressed man behind him. "He's not here," there was confusion and disbelief on her face.

"Could you tell us where we might contact him?"

Just then another woman in her late thirties joined the others in the doorway.

"What's up mum?"

"These men are looking for your father."

"Can we come in?" the Senior Constable showed his badge. Officialdom always cleared the way, the two women stood aside.

"Come through."

There was no money here, Athol who had said nothing so far thought as they were lead through to the kitchen.

"What's he done?" Mrs. Horsley asked.

"Oh nothing," the Senior Constable was handling the situation.

"We would like to talk to Mr. Horsley about the car he bought from a Mrs. Johnson."

"We don't know where he is," Mrs. Horsley looked at her daughter, who said.

"No."

"And you are Mr. Horsley's daughter?"

"Yes."

"Is there anyone else in the house?" the questioning continued. 'What's that got to do with anything?' Athol D'Large who had still added nothing to this part of the investigation thought.

"No, mum passed last year, God rest her soul."

"I'm sorry to hear that." The Senior Constable nodded his condolences. Athol D'Large looked at the floor and rubbed his forehead.

"You would have liked her, God rest her soul."

The cop nodded.

"So you don't know where your husband is?" he asked realizing nothing was working.

"We haven't seen him for months. He doesn't know mum's dead, God rest her soul."

"Can anyone tell us where he is?"

"He's got two brothers living at the end of the Street."

"Oh, can you elaborate on that?"

"Number 115."

"Thank you."

"If you find him tell him not to come back," were Emit's wife's last words.

"I like the way you worked that interview." Athol D'Large praised the Officer as the car moved off to their next prospect."

"Bad luck about the mother," he hesitated, "God rests her soul."

Donald Horsley answered the door at number 115 Bulwer Street and was as surprised about the interest the police had in his brother as he had always been about his sudden disappearance. "When we hadn't seen him for a month, Albert here," Donald looked at his brother, "and I went to his house."

"So you weren't close?' It was Athol D'Large who was asking the questions this time.

"No," Donald rested and then his brother took over. "We used to see Emit sometimes down at the Bowling Club, but after not seeing him for about a month, we went to see her."

"Her being the wife?" Athol D'Large continued.

"Yes," Albert looked the well-dressed interviewer in the eye, "have you met her?"

"Yes she gave us your address."

"No wonder he left."

"You don't think they got on?" the questioning wasn't leading to a conclusion, it was more a conversation.

"Who could," Donald joined back into the conversation, "her, the daughter and the mother."

"God rest her soul." Athol D'Large couldn't help himself.

"Yeah I heard she passed," Donald showed no sympathy.

"Do you blokes want a beer?" Albert asked.

It was a bit early, but clearly these fellows wanted to talk. "Thanks," Athol D'Large looked at the Senior Constable.

"Sure thing."

The four men walked through the sparsely furnished house to the back verandah, where there were a few old couches and a refrigerator humming away on a side wall. "Pull up a pew," Albert walked to the ancient cooling appliance and opened the door wide.

"W'attle it be boys?" The grammar suited the man and his machine and the proud assortment of every beverage.

"You wouldn't have a Tooheys in there would you?" asked Athol. "We got it all."

"Is that a Hahn I see?" the Senior Constable lit up.

"Good choice," the barman judged, as he grabbed two Westies for his brother and himself "I don't go much on the Tooheys."

"You've got to live there," Athol D'Large defended his state and the state beer.

"This is Athol D'Large the Sydney A League footballer."

"Look I knew that name when you introduced yourself, when are you going to pull the boots on?" Albert was now fully enthused.

"I'm over here to work. I like it here though, maybe one day I will play for you people."

"We need help." replied Albert.

"You've got good management Albert, now that's what makes a team work." Athol D'Large gave a little professional insight into the league.

"Your brother Emit," Athol D'Large turned the conversation now it was on a favourable note. "Do you have any idea where he could have gone?"

"As far away from her as he could," Donald chipped in.

"He bought a car, a real nice Statesman. Brought it around here one day didn't he Albert?"

"Yeah, you know," Albert replied. "I think that was the last time we saw him."

"Did the police investigate?" Athol D'Large went down the formal path.

"Oh yeah," it was Donald's turn, "but a month had gone by, you know she never said a word, by then the track had gone cold."

"So what were the findings?" Athol pursued with his questions.

"The cops said he shot through. Who could blame him, I reckon they should have charged her with obstructing justice."

"Lots of people disappear every day," Athol tried to make the situation easier by generalizing. "Kids leave home, usually for what they conceive as freedom. Husbands as you depict, leave wives because of incompatibility. Some just don't fit in to the environment that they find themselves in. You don't know where he could have gone?" The well-dressed Prosecutor pushed on.

Donald looked at the man delving deeply into his brother's disappearance. "Are you two from missing persons?"

"No, but we need to talk to your brother."

"Why do you need to talk to Emit now, after all this time?" Donald started to probe.

"It's to do with that car you just mentioned." Athol played it down.

"The Statesman?" Albert the other brother queried.

"Yes."

"Why is it stolen?"

"No, we think it was involved in a case we're looking into." Neither of the brothers seemed convinced.

"He didn't give a hint to where he might go?" Athol could see these two brothers clamming up to protect their sibling.

"Nothing I'm sorry we can't help you."

The two law men thanked the Horsley brothers for the beer and left.

"What now?" Senior Constable Davies asked. "We're drawing blanks."

"Well those two fellows are now very sceptical and the wife is a disillusioned negative," Athol D'Large summed up the situation, "but we have to find Emit Horsley, did you notice a shed or garage at his house?"

"No I can't recall seeing one; I think it was a narrow block."

"I'll drive by again and try not to get noticed."

"Why don't we go back to them and tell them we need to search the shed, if they refuse to let us in, we can always get a search warrant?" Michael said.

"No we can't."

"I don't understand." Michael Davies looked at his superior.

"This is not an official case," Athol paused, "yet."

Michael said nothing.

Athol D'Large drove past the home of the mother and daughter they interviewed a couple of hours earlier. "Do you see a garage there?" he asked.

"No, oh hang on, I see a roof up the back, but there is no side driveway."

"Maybe there is rear access; we'll go around the block."

There was a narrow lane at the back of the corner house.

"Voila."

"Pardon me."

"Rear access; see if you can pick the garage from this side."

The car cruised up the narrow lane.

"Voila." Senior Constable used his new word as he pointed to an iron roof behind a high corrugated fence. Athol drove to the end of the lane into the street and parked.

"I think this is what's called a grey area Senior Constable," the Prosecutor turned to his offsider.

"I need to look in that garage. I have a feeling about Emit Horsley and that car. You stay here I'll check it out."

"I'll come, I don't get much excitement."

"This is not just unofficial, it's illegal." Athol explained.

"I know I've read the book,' the offsider laughed. "I learned something today."

"Yes, what's that?"

"Never stop looking."

"That's right." Athol got out of the car and spoke over the roof. "Nobody told us anything today, whether they didn't want to or just didn't know. Either way we could go back with nothing. See what the garage holds."

The men could see the back of the house from the gate, there was one window probably a kitchen. The gate was easy. Once they were at the door of the garage they were shielded from the house. The door was locked. Athol twisted and pulled the round knob, it came off in his hand. The men heard the door handle and the whole lock mechanism fall on the inside of the garage. He looked at the knob in his hand and suppressed a laugh. The rickety door came open.

It was a one car accommodative structure; some light came in from a window over a work bench, more light sifted in between the cracks of the shrunken weather boards. Athol went to the window it had direct line of sight to the sole window of the house. No movement down there.

As the men's eyes became accustomed to the dim light it was obvious the door on this place hadn't been opened for some time, probably not since Emit Horsley left. Cobwebs surprised them more than once and in the semi dark they had to be careful where they put their feet. Athol noticed four storage boxes stacked neatly on the bench with a generous coating of dust on them. He lifted one to inspect its contents but its weight told him that had been removed. He tore off the lid with the self-storage name on it. "Now we have something. When we get back to the car have a look at that directory I'll bet the Street on this self-storage box top runs off Bayswater Road."

"And look at this." Michael showed the Prosecutor?? a magazine with half of the second page ripped off. The heading read: 'Beautiful Shoal Bay the game fishing capital of the East Coast.'

"Let's go." Athol took a quick look out the window; they were both out the door and in the lane in twenty seconds.

"Voila." Senior Constable Davies had this new language down pat.

"John Johnson was either putting something into the storage shed or taking it out."

"So we check out the storage shed." The Senior Constable was getting right into this case.

"No we check out the car at, where was that place again?'

The Policeman opened the magazine, "Shoal Bay."

CHAPTER 27

CLOSING IN

A phone rang in the pocket of a sports jacket left in the change shed of an inner Sydney sports oval. It rang again.

The third time the caller left a message.

"You're either at training or you're at training. This is Athol. Please ring me."

It was an hour before the message was retrieved.

"Athol it's Kevin are you ready to come back and play football?"

"No that's not what the call's about. I've got a job for you if you're interested."

"Sure, you want me to do some snooping for you?"

"Yes, but not on the computer. Shoal Bay, that's in Port Stephens isn't it?"

"Sure is, I know it well."

"This could be the big one. When you get home type in 'The Daily Clearance Case', I've got a lead on it. Ring me back. Keep it quiet."

"Yeah ok I'm nearly home I'll read it and ring you in an hour."

It was almost seven in the evening when the phone rang on Athol D'Large's desk. He saw the number.

"Kevin."

"Hey, I'm looking at this clearance case deal. It has me intrigued. Is this real money or play money?"

"Funny you should ask that," Athol laughed, "it is play money in that it was created out of currency exchange shuffling, but it is hard cash when you do the sums."

"I'm on the computer are you near one?"

"Yes I'm in the office."

The computer wiz went into IT talk. "Go to Team, bring up the file, and show me how it worked."

"Ok I met with a guy named George Hennesy from the Federal Police." Athol explained as he followed his friend's instructions on the computer program.

"They had a team of outside auditors go through all the transactions at Daily Clearance that John Johnson handled. Out of the," he couldn't guess "I don't know how many, there were fourteen that had their currencies changed out of and back to their currency of origin. It was the last fourteen deals that Johnson handled. Does that tell you something?" Athol asked his friend.

"No."

"He worked out how to do it," Athol prompted, "and he did it every time after that."

"Of course," Kevin reacted, "now show me the how."

"Right, the last case was not finished; we'll come back to that. Go to the one before." Athol explained.

"The Trade Deal IN-239 it was an Indian Australian trade deal which was an iron ore contract between Atcom Resources and Shallah Steel Mills to deliver four hundred thousand tonnes of ore at ninety-eight dollars per tonne by the seventeenth of September."

"Got it." Kevin followed

"There is a twenty eight day contract lull period where the money is in suspense, so it is not settled until the fifteenth of October."

"I see."

"The Federal Police Officer George Hennesy and his team did a great job of tracking the deal. Click on currency graphs," Athol lead Kevin through the course, "then click Rupee, US dollar in the period seventeenth September to twenty first September."

"Yes I see that," Kevin said, "thirty nine million US dollars."

"Now on the twenty first September there is a switch to the British Pound." Athol lead Kevin through the maze. "By the twenty eighth September there is a surplus of three hundred and ten thousand dollars."

"What!" Athol could imagine the look on his friends face. "What does he do now besides buy a Maserati?"

"He seals the deal by buying the US dollar equivalent of the rupee for the contracted amount."

"What about the surplus?"

"Go down to appendix, a gold contract is bought in the name of Smyth Sons nominees to the value of three hundred and ten thousand dollars US."

"And you think Smyth Sons nominees is this Johnson character."

"Well Smyth could be a synonym of Smith; there are a few of them. If you are going to pick a name."

"So now Smyth Sons nominees have three hundred and ten thousand dollars in gold?" Kevin Tucker asked.

"Yes, gold is the standard which most trading countries use to cover their cash holdings, its price doesn't swing like currencies unless something bad happens like a war or some financial crisis. But you know this."

"I do, now you have got me. When you buy gold they don't come around to your place with a wheel barrow full. You get a contract as you would with shares, only its world standard, and set in US dollars held by all federal reserves the world over." There was a long pause, Athol waited.

"I've got it," Kevin said, "this man of yours was also head of Bank Note Rejuvenation, and he simply changes gold contracts for old notes through the Federal Reserve."

"That's how he did it. " Athol was relieved.

"But," there was another long pause, "this guy died. Do you think he died and went to Shoal Bay?"

"No." The laughter from Perth could be heard in Sydney and vice versa. "There's another character."

"Oh, and you think he's got the money, and he's the guy I've got to find in Shoal bay."

"Yes."

The two colleagues went over everything compiling a workable computer file.

Emit Horsley had not existed. He hadn't filed a tax return, his Medicare card had not been presented his license had expired and his credit card was cancelled. "He doesn't want to be found." Kevin Tucker said.

"No, but he would have created a new identity. And as you and I know from past cases, ill-gotten riches don't stay concealed long. It's the spending that gives them away."

With football and training commitments it was Monday of the next week before Kevin Tucker could get up to Shoal Bay. It was still the gem in the crown that was Port Stephens. Only a couple of hours out of Sydney Kevin knew the pleasures of 'The Bay.'

CHAPTER 28

RETRIEVING THE TREASURE

"I just spoke to Steve," Sandy Horder called out from the deck of the cruiser moored on the wharf at Hawks Nest. "We'll go back in the morning."

"Look at this," Muscat and Dominic had become friendly with the local fishermen and bought something each day from their morning catch. The big Italian reached into a wet hessian bag and picked out a good size crab. "How will that go with a white wine for lunch?"

Sandy patted his belly, "I've got to get back to doing something."

It was seven o'clock when Sandy and the boys of the *Sugar Bay* were attracted by five men waving from the unfamiliar landing spot at Sandy Point. Steve had secured the use of the private jetty earlier in the week, he needed somewhere to load.

Muscat pointed.

"I see," Sandy steered a corrected course.

"What's that cage doing?" Dominic the man of few words confused his utterance again.

Sandy, one hand on the wheel picked up his binoculars. "Looks like a steel cage."

All was revealed in a few minutes after vigorous handshaking. "Shark protection," Steve explained "it was Jimmy's idea, don't ask where it came from."

"It's to put the diamonds in, we don't want the sharks eating them," Jimmy joked.

"I'm not asking where it came from," Sandy said "let's get it on board."

****

DERRICK FULLERTON SAT on the beautiful Dutchies Beach every morning from dawn. He knew the *Sugar Bay* was further up the reaches of Port Stephens somewhere, and if they wanted to put to sea, there was only one way. They had to come past Dutchies. At seven forty that morning he spotted her, there was something big covered over on the deck. Derrick knew they were headed for the treasure he also knew the big Norwegian salvage operator would be waiting.

They were.

"Hey Boss, I think I see what you're looking for," yelled the overweight unkempt deck hand, who Gunnar Hagen kept around. Handy when things got rough on the boat, handy when things got rough on the street.

"I see it looks like they're rigged this time."

"Shark protection?"

"I wouldn't go down without it, I might send you down, but I wouldn't."

"Yeah, 'coarse." The big and ugly faked a laugh.

Gunnar Hagen had a reputation for just being bad. Don't test him.

"We goin' after 'em?" the seaman asked.

"I know where they're headed."

★★★★★★★★★★

"THAT'S THE BLOODY old salvage," Maurice said when Shoal Bay came into view.

"Yes replied Sandy from the bridge, I thought they would have packed up by now."

"What's the plan?" Steve was on the bridge, he was keen to go.

Sandy looked straight to the heads. "We'll go to the spot, give it an hours fishing. If we're not interrupted and you're right with it, you can go down."

"Good."

★★★★★★★★★★

THAT NIGHT A FLAT nosed aluminium dinghy was pushed into the white topped ripple on a black night off the beach at Shoal Bay, down from the Country Club. Sandy got the bottoms of his expensive rolled up chinos wet as he ran behind the small craft and jumped in. He looked into the dark water of the bay to sharpen his night vision, then took up the oars and rowed to the target.

The sounds back at the bay dimmed as Sandy Horder closed in on his objective. She was bigger up close, more than twice the size of the *Sugar Bay*, and she was rough. She was a rugged old working salvage and she was the enemy.

Sandy Horder wanted to keep the pressure on the crew. He knew what they were here for. He knew they knew he knew. At the end of the night attention would be brought to the fact.

Sandy rowed slowly around the vessel and under the cover of the slopping bow and located the fore and aft anchor ropes.

He attached a small plastic bag on each, and then he looked for a point to board. She sat higher out of the water than the *Sugar Bay* and the only way on was by the anchor ropes. He loosely tied the dinghy to it thinking of a quick getaway and tried his hand at hand over hand rope climbing. He struggled that last metre and clambered aboard. His was grateful for the dim light there. The muffled sound of a generator was all he could hear. Sandy looked down at the dinghy for security. A door opened; there was a sound of voices below. A large figure stepped onto the deck, emptied the last of a bottle into his mouth, made a couple of bodily noises and threw the bottle overboard. The door opened again. Sandy guessed this was the Captain as soon as he opened his mouth.

"You're a pig Hennesy."

"Said daddy pig to little pig."

'She's gonna be on' Sandy thought, 'I'd better get in first.' With that he jumped from his crouched position and went in with the shoulder waist high. The big man with his back to the rail cracked two ribs as he, the Captain and Sandy flew over the side. The big hit, the surprise and the cold water had the crew members scrambling for life and crying for help. Sandy swam to the dinghy and slipped quietly away.

It was a full five minutes before the rest of the crew got the ropes and life buoys to the disabled seamen. Sandy was almost back when he took a toggle switch from a plastic bag. Both ends of the old salvage were rocked with a bang.

Sandy showed that he was in control once again.

✦✦✦✦✦✦✦✦✦

DERRICK WATCHED FROM THE seat in front of The Country Club as the stack behind the wheelhouse of the salvage boat belched its first cloud of carbon dioxide for the day.

"They all have to come back, I'll be waiting," he said to Bruno.

It was nearly nine when Walt and Jimmy pulled the green tarpaulin over the bridge of the *Sugar Bay* to break up the outline and to camouflage her.

"Are you happy with this?" Sandy asked Steve, referring to the make shift shark cage.

"Yes Jimmy did a good job. He picked it up from a building site, strengthened it with these concrete reinforcement bars made the door with a 'D' coupling lock. Nothing can get me in here."

"How's it looking up there Maurice?" Sandy called to the bridge.

"All's quiet, nothing on the horizon." The old man reported.

"Are you sure you're right Steve?" Sandy asked needing to be reassured.

"I'll have the cord on at all times." Steve tied the communication rope to his wrist.

The three men lifted the make shift cage to the back of the boat and lowered it into the water. Steve Flint dropped in and pulled the door over securing it with the 'D' bolt. He nodded to Sandy and grabbed the rope on his wrist. This was his life line.

Weightlessness took over as the cage drifted down to the sunken cruiser. Steve felt safe, he enjoyed the scenery. He watched as the current moved the sea plants like a slow motion breeze, schools of small fish changed direction and darted as one. He was coming into a calm paradise; he did the 360 degree scan before he opened the door and manipulated the cage onto the sunken cruiser's deck. Once in place he gave the communication rope two distinctive tugs.

"He's there," a relieved Sandy told the crew around him, he looked up to give Maurice, who stood lookout on the bridge, the thumbs up. Maurice in return waved the all clear.

CHAPTER 29

THE NET TIGHTENS

Kevin Tucker pulled the little A4 Audi into a spot just up from the Country Club at nine on Monday morning. He had made the booking at the landmark retreat soon after the phone call from Athol D'Large.

"You have three days off?" Athol had asked. "It shouldn't be hard for you."

"No," Kevin replied, "just find a guy by the name of Emit Horsley who doesn't use his real name."

"Same old thing," the Prosecutor had joked, "usual suspects in big cars and a cruiser or two moored in the bay."

Kevin walked across the road to the large main entrance of the Country Club.

"Ah they're moving that salvage boat," an old gentleman in a linen jacket and a neatly trimmed moustache said as he bumped into Kevin at the glass doors.

"I'm sorry," it was more of a confused apology to the old man.

"The salvage boat," he pointed out.

Kevin followed the extended arm and finger. "I see," he smiled, "so this is a big thing?" Two men who had been sitting on a bench facing the bay stood up.

"It's been sitting there for a week. They say she's been commissioned to bring up an old wreck."

"You'll have to keep me informed." Kevin moved into the foyer. The old man walked out on to the street where he would spread his message further.

"Do you have off street parking?" Kevin Tucker asked the girl on reception.

"Yes we do, the access is from the rear. The button on your room key will open the gate Mr. Tucker, and there's a lift to your floor."

"Thanks."

Kevin Tucker walked out of the hotel and across the road to his car. The two men he noticed earlier looking out at the bay now stood at the fence observing the salvage boat.

'A lot of interest there,' he thought.

Once in the underground car park Kevin Tucker found his allocated spot not far from the entrance, he backed the Audi in and locked it with his remote. The majority of empty spaces told the man from Sydney that he was an early arrival for the weekend stayers. As with all resort accommodation these units would be privately owned but managed by the Country Club. At the far end of the quite large underground space was the lock up area. Individual car spaces divided by chain wire fencing, accessed through a roller door. This was where the owner occupiers and long -time stayers kept their stuff.

There was a BMW, a tinnie on a boat trailer, a couple of the obligatory jet-skies and an old car. Kevin Tucker took a closer look.

A Maroon Statesman.

★★★★★★★★★★

SANDY HORDER SAT on the edge of the padded seat port side, the communication rope tied to his wrist. He stared at the parallax bend where the rope went through the water and knew that life would never be the same again with or without the sunken treasure. He had an uneasy insecure feeling. Not only did he have Derrick Fullerton to contend with. The salvage operator could be another threat. The life Sandy Horder had made for himself could be closing in on him.

Down below Steve Flint left the security of the mew makeshift shark protection cage and made his way back to the Captain's suite via the narrow stair from the bridge. In the safe confines of the cage he had taken the communication rope off and had systematically searched the suite. Apart from odd trinkets in the desk drawers nothing was turned up.

He was missing something. There must have been more than the diamonds in the drawer. There has to be a cache somewhere. He retrieved the rope and swam back up the narrow stairs to the bridge. This is where it happened, the shoot out and subsequent explosion.

He looked at the gaping hole in the deck straight through to the sea bed. It must have been some explosion. This ex-military man wondered why the whole thing didn't go up. It had to have been planned. The Captain set the explosives, gave out the co-ordinates and pulled the pin. He must have known of an impending mutiny set up the explosives under the engines and goodbye.

Steve Flint swam to the steps that lead to the main deck making sure not to snare the life line. There were three other suites on this level and they were two steps down from the

Captain's, which had its own deck, and as Steve discovered, private access to the bridge.

The first suite next to the Captain's was a saloon, board room. Steve left the rope at the door to investigate. The room was done out as was the Captain's suite, wood panelling, lounge type chairs and a mirrored bar along a side wall. The sea had rotted and warped the timber, the crannies and gaps were homes for all sorts of finned and legged creatures, who surprised the diver unexpectedly after he turned up in their domain.

He stood in the middle of the room. This would be a likely spot for a safe, or a concealed cupboard. He pulled panelling off where he could, and searched behind the bar. There were cabinets for display, but nothing said impregnable.

He left the room, checked all round for any danger, took hold of the life line and swam back up to the bridge deck. Steve didn't know what he was looking for, but still felt he was onto something. His tank gave its first warning he should make his way back up.

He turned to head back to the cage and caught sight of a heavy looking chest in the mangled hole that was the engine bay. He swam down, his blood turned cold, nervousness and excitement hit him almost to the point of passing out. Steve let the life line go and grabbed a handle on the side of the chest, it wouldn't move. Heavy beams from the boats framework had it entrapped. There was only one way, he took the life line and kicked hard with his flippers. A small shark at the entrance of the hole was pushed aside with the butt of his gun. Two more sharks appeared at the stairs to the lower deck.

Steve had blood pumping through his body at ten times the normal rate. He was going to get to the cage, get what he needed and come back. He swam towards the first shark, flicked the safety on the gun and felt the recoil on the charged spear. The second predator had a change of heart. Steve swam to the cage secured the door with the 'D' bolt and pulled the life line twice.

"He's coming up," a worried Sandy said, he hadn't taken his eye off the communication rope since Steve the diver went down. This whole treasure hunt was beginning to question Sandy Horder's values. He had never been happier. He had respect and position in a community and true valued friends. Now he was putting himself up against a criminal element. Mr. Cool had it all why did it have to be jeopardized?

All that his true valued friends wanted to do was fish, now they're talking about sunken treasure on the high seas. There was old Maurice Campbell up on the bridge keeping an eye out for the enemy. Steve's coming up from below where he's been mixing with sharks. The rest of the crew were taking turns to pull the cage up by hand using a couple of chains. 'What if someone got hurt?'

The cage broke the surface; Steve was out and clawing for the boat.

"Are you alright?" This was the breaking point for Sandy; he could see Steve was panicked.

Muscat got the handover grip on Steve's freehand and pulled him onto the rear landing. The diver hunched his shoulders and gasped.

"I've found it! I found the treasure!"

"He found it!" Muscat the big Italian jumped for joy with his friend Dominic and rejoiced as only Italians can.

"What did you find?" Walt McEnroe yelled excitedly, he desperately needed more information. Sandy stood back to let it all unfold.

On his feet now and still pumping blood at a dangerous rate Steve undid his tank. "The treasure chest. Jimmy could you get me the other tank?"

"You're not going back down?" Sandy questioned.

"Yep. Now we need the explosives, the big ones, and another charged spear."

"You encountered another shark?" Walt asked.

"Yep."

"Rest up a bit, have a cup of tea." Sandy was concerned at Steve's agitation.

On Sandy's insistence the men sat around the railings of the *Sugar Bay* on the padded seats. Sandy wanted to get the number one diver talking, to get him to unwind. "Tell us what you found," he said.

"I think it was all set up," Steve said leaning forward, resting his elbows on his knees, he was piecing it together. "The Captain's suite was under the bridge. The engines were below that. Now I searched the Captain's suite, and the saloon, boardroom area looking for a safe, couldn't find anything. I thought that was strange. Now it all comes together. What nationality was he, this Captain?" Steve looked at Muscat looking for an answer.

"Dunno."

"I think he had a great attachment to his special cargo," Steve went on, "he must have had it hidden behind a wall in his suite. Now as I said the suite was next to the bridge, the engine compartment directly below. The Captain could have set explosives down there as an insurance he guarded the treasure with his life."

"So if he couldn't have it?" Sandy Horder stepped in.

"Or whoever commissioned this very elaborate shipment wanted to ensure it didn't fall into the wrong hands." Steve Flint added.

"It was suicide." Maurice Campbell said gruffly.

"Maybe it was the last stand in a long battle, could have been a stray bullet that set the explosion off." Walt McEnroe was talking his audience through the last frames of a TV Western.

"So the explosion loosened the treasure chest from the hiding place?" Sandy asked.

"Yes." Steve was definite.

"How do we get it out?" Jimmy Zininski was all for going in now.

"Or should we?" Sandy wanted to give his friends something to think over.

"What do you mean?" It was Jimmy again.

"Respect the Captain's wishes and leave it where he put it."

"No." the old farmer from up in the Valley was first to respond. "We have come a long way, it was an adventure and we have found it we've got to bring it up."

Dick Walker and Walt McEnroe always stuck together.

"Yes it's ours," Walt spoke for everyone.

"Of course," Dick agreed.

The other two looked at Sandy. Sandy in turn looked at the two Italians.

"I know we had an agreement but I know what you want Muscat."

"I'd like to see it go home." Muscat responded.

CHAPTER 30

THE LAST DIVE

The phone rang in Athol D'Large's pocket as he walked down the steps of the State Office block in the Perth CBD.

He'd had a two hour meeting with the Police Commissioner who was very pleased with the acute and definitive way he had closed the Selby Securities saga. It had all the trimmings a failing government needed. News coverage, two of the highest ranking business leaders in the State in custody awaiting hearing, and the first man contracted into the State Justice System to clean up a mess. Athol D'Large was that man.

"Kevin how is the holiday going?"

"Swimmingly."

"Oh good I'm glad you're enjoying it, nice weather?" Athol inquired.

"No swimmingly, I mean, I may have something. That car, was it a maroon earlier model Statesman?"

"I believe so. Have you found it?"

"Well I'm staying at the Country Club and there's one like it in a lock up here."

"Did you say the Country Club?" Athol stopped in his tracks, a questioned frown formed on his brow. "I'm sure that was the name of place we saw on the magazine in his garage."

"It's the biggest place in town," Kevin said. "They built it before they built the bay."

"Yes that's it alright, 'When you're over on the east coast visit The Country Club.'" Athol quoted.

"As I said it's in a lookup we need to get the VIN number to check with your copy of the registration."

"Yes this sounds good," Athol was thinking on his feet. "If it's been registered in New South Wales, we'll have the new owner's name."

"It is a secure lookup, but it only has a roller door on it." Kevin was working on his next move.

"Don't get caught."

****

SANDY WAS ON the bridge of the *Sugar Bay* with the binoculars. He had searched all around then concentrated on the exaggerated arc of the course that brought them to this spot. There was nothing. He thought the salvage boat would have followed.

"Sandy's worried." Maurice said to Steve.

"Yes, but we're so close." The diver didn't look up as he joined wires that were attached to a bundle of explosives.

"I shouldn't talk to you while you're doing this," Maurice said.

"It's ok." The diver wrapped some tape around the last joint. The rest of the crew stood up next to the bridge the furthest point from the explosives without going to the upper fore deck. Distance is only a psychological safety barrier with explosives. If this thing did go off on the deck there would only be smoke on the water. "Sandy," Steve looked up to the bridge.

"Right," Sandy took his time descending the three steps. "Are you sure you're right with this?" he asked reassuring himself.

"Sandy," Steve got up and put his hand on the Sandy's shoulder, "you know we don't want the riches this will bring. Let's do what our friends want to do, send it home. But," he added "we've got to bring it up first."

It was another hour before Steve was ready with the explosives and he and Jimmy had rigged a couple of chains to lift the chest once it had been released from the wreck's grasp. The weather, always the seaman's uncertainty was closing in from the south. The gathering dark clouds, Sandy thought would cut down on visibility if the salvage boat was out there looking. And he knew it would be out there looking.

"How long do you estimate Steve?" Sandy looked at the clouds.

"I'll go and set the explosives, come back up, we move off the sight. Press the button. We go back, I go down fix the gear then we pull her up."

"How long?"

"Hour and a half tops."

"Ok let's go."

"The weather forecast doesn't predict anything nasty," Steve reassured Sandy as he looked skyward, "I wouldn't go down if it did."

"No I was thinking more of a cover," Sandy replied.

"I know what you mean," Steve looked to the horizon. "That salvage could be a mile off us on a grey afternoon, and with this camouflage he wouldn't see us."

The crew on deck took turns on the chains as the cage with its extra weight of rigging gear was lowered down to the sunken cruiser. Steve looked at the bones of the once beautiful craft knowing there wouldn't be much left after his next decent. He undid the 'D' bolt and manoeuvred the cage onto the deck. He grabbed as much gear as he could leaving the gun and the communication rope. The excitement was growing again. He swam down into the hole. There she was. He looked at the chest as if it was his life's work, his legacy. He placed the few chains he could carry and all the explosives on the chest, allowed himself a few seconds glory, and then swam out of the hole to go back to the cage for the remainder of the gear.

All the excitement that had been building since the decent was replaced with fear when he saw the shark with its head inside the safety cage. Once it sensed movement the grey terror of the deep swung around to face the adversary and knocked the cage off the deck which in turn pulled the chain hard on the hands of those on the deck of the *Sugar Bay* still holding it, waiting for the all clear on the communication rope.

"What was that?" Jimmy looked at Muscat.

The caged pulled the chains again as it bumped on the side of the cruiser then dropped to the ocean floor.

"What's going on down there?"

This was Sandy Horder's worst night-mare.

"Pull it up." He stood, handed the communication rope to Maurice Campbell and jumped to the edge of the deck landing to help with the lifting. The cage broke the surface.

"It's empty." Sandy leaned out and pulled the makeshift safety module closer to the boat. The gun still in the cage triggered Sandy into action.

"Jimmy get the other gear."

"You're not going down."

"Get the gear."

"You can't go down there." Maurice said. "You've never done this before."

Sandy had his shoes and shirt off.

"Give me a hand." He ordered, and took the tank from the younger man.

In two minutes Sandy looked something like a deep sea diver. He got into the cage and picked up the gun.

"How does this go?" He held the weapon up for Muscat.

"Safety forward she's ready," he pointed to Sandy's mouthpiece. "Two deep breaths."

Fearlessly Sandy nodded to the crew and pointed down tightening the "D' bolt up as he descended.

Before he was half way down Sandy was struggling with the air. He pulled the mouthpiece out. The air escaped, he tried again limiting his breaths this worked better. He looked up, and the underside of his beloved cruiser was disappearing from view. He looked down, still trying to work this face mask and breathing apparatus out, into nothing.

Time slowed, the unknown pushed his heart rate up. He held the gun tight. He peered straight down for fear he would lose his landing place. There it was directly below.

Sandy hadn't realized the communication rope was wrapped around a bar in the cage.

Why?

At the same time Gunner Hagen was slowly manoeuvring his vessel from the coordinates that he had to the spot he thought the *Sugar Bay* would be – the spot where they hurriedly left on their last encounter. About a 2 or 3 kilometre area.

His old sea weathered vessel at slow speed also had the advantage of blending in with the grey overcast conditions.

It was the young lookout on the forward crane that picked out the partially concealed form of the smart 28 foot cruiser. "Pull ahead 1 - 2 kilometres," he called.

"We've got the bastards," Gunner looked up to the forward crane, spun the wheel for direction and eased on the power. The big diesels belched their black smoke and growled at the otherwise stillness.

Maurice, on the bridge of the *Sugar Bay* , looking above the camouflaged tarp was the first alerted. "We've been spotted," he raised the big gun.

"No, Maurice….." Jimmy left his post of chain puller and raced to the steps of the bridge. He jumped on the third one and pulled himself up alongside the old man and grabbed the barrel. They both stared at the fresh black smoke coming towards them. The four on the deck below pointed helplessly at the danger coming. Six men caught, six men to face their nemesis without their leader. They stood and watched horrified as the salvage pulled up alongside.

As Sandy was lowered closer he looked around his prison, the explosives and the chains the boys had fashioned as a lifting cradle were gone. So Steve needed two hands. He was probably fixing the explosives right now.

The cage stopped abruptly on the ocean floor stirring the fine sand which rose up as a mist. When Sandy took the 'D' bolt off and dropped the cage door, another cloud of cover puffed up, enough to attract the attention of the shark that had Steve bailed up in the hole. It turned and darted in the direction of the cage giving its prisoner Steve time to escape. Once in the open Steve could see Sandy, who had come to save him, unaware of the danger that was coming at him from above.

"Shoot," Steve spat out the mouthpiece.

Sandy spotted Steve and the rising bubbles through the restricted view of the diving mask, instinct turned him up and to the left. The Grey 12 foot terror saw Sandy as easy prey in the open and honed in on him.

Steve watched as Sandy kicked hard with the flippers and tore at the water with his left hand. The shark's jaws opened. Man and beast eyed each other for that last moment in time.

Mechanics took over. The right thumb touched the safety at the same time the index finger pulled hard on the trigger.

The monster stopped, rolled and fell in gracious slow motion. Steve propelled through the dark red murky water. They were both in trouble now. With no shots left Steve bundled Sandy still holding the gun and pushed him into the back of the cage and crouched down in front of him, the door couldn't close.

Two smaller sharks came through the red shadow and fearlessly attacked the opening. Steve prodded the first one with the butt of the empty gun, then put his hand through the mesh and violently pulled the communication rope. Immediately the cage rose and the two game fish retreated to the bloodied carcass on the sea floor.

Steve reloaded the gun from the auxiliary pack under the barrel on the way up. He and Sandy were hedging on mental exhaustion but maintained the vigilant alertness instilled by fear.

They were almost to the surface when they both realized they were headed to the underside of two hulls not one, and knew they were being dragged into yet more danger.

"Welcome aboard." Gunner Hager the Norwegian salvage Captain greeted a still shell shocked Steve as he was lifted onto the rear landing of the *Sugar Bay* .

"You have been treasure hunting." It was the sickly smile of the under achieved.

Sandy stepped out from behind Steve; he aimed the gun straight at the unwanted raider.

"Get off my boat."

The intruder froze. Time stopped. There was no option.

The adrenalin that pumped Sandy up in dire situations kicked in with anger. He lifted his right flipper enhanced foot and slapped it down on the deck moving forward, at the same time levelling the gun at Gunner Hager's face.

The rugged Norwegian stared at the eyes in the mask and retreated, enticing his two backups to do the same.

"Jump!" Sandy shouted when his captives were at the rail of the *Sugar Bay* closest to the salvage vessel. He held the gun a meter from the face of the man who broke the primary law of the sea.

"Jump!"

Sandy Horder never took his eyes off his opposing Captain and kept the gun aimed at him even as he climbed into the wheel house. A puff of black smoke belched from the stack, the rough looking vessel edged away.

"They won't be back today," Sandy stated with confidence, he made the gun safe and laid it on the starboard seat.

"Let's get this job finished," Steve was on his feet.

"You're not going down there again?" Walt pointed out there and looked at Sandy for support.

"We will leave it for another day." Sandy said taking off his mask.

"I don't think I could come back to this place," Steve didn't make a move to remove any of his gear, "after what happened today I'm nearly ready to cut my ties with the sea." Steve looked at the men through his fogged mask. "This man saved me. I had 10 minutes of air left, trapped down the hole by a shark. We all owe this man a life or two and our lives now revolve around this chest."

Maurice stepped into the debate; as usual his thoughts were of care and support, delivered in a tactful way. "You have the hardest most dangerous job Steve. Maybe you should rest a day or two, and then come back."

Steve just looked at the old man. "No," Steve shook his head and pointed to Sandy, "this man saved my life down there, I've got to go back and finish the job."

"We could leave it there." Sandy was in charge but kept the conversation going with an option.

"No." Steve wanted to see it through.

"What's your plan?" Sandy asked.

The men gathered around Steve Flint, he pushed his mask up. "I've set the blast up to the back in a way that it should blow out, thus exposing the chest. The cradle has been fixed."

Steve then went through the steps. "We move the boat off the site, blow the wreck, set up back here again and then I go down hook up the chain and we pull her up. One hour tops."

"That weather is changing, but we've got a good hour."

Steve looked at the sky.

"If I thought the weather was a problem I wouldn't go down."

"We had better get going." Sandy headed for the bridge. "There is another tank down there isn't there Jimmy?"

"No" said Steve "by my estimation we both have only about half left."

****

KEVIN TUCKER GOT OUT of the lift at basement level and nervously looked around, he hurried to the lockup area where he pulled a screwdriver from his pocket and inserted it into the lock of the second door down. He gave it a twist clockwise, and then the reverse, nothing happened. Instinctively and out of fear of being caught the novice burglar pressed down on the bottom ledge to take the load off the lock slides and twisted the screwdriver anticlockwise again. He heard the lock mechanism hit the concrete floor on the inside.

Relief passed fear as he entered the lockup. The door was hurriedly pulled down. The lift bell rang, Kevin, who had just started taking down the particulars from the registration sticker, ducked for cover behind the car. A couple walked to the lockup next to where he was hiding.

There was the familiar fiddling with the lock, the keys fell to the ground, there was a bit of mumblings about the bad light, then. "Hey look Sandy's door isn't closed properly." A female voice said.

Kevin froze, his first thought was to rush them and make a run for it.

"Shit let's get out of here, they might still be in there." The boyfriend showed his colours.

Five minutes later Kevin Tucker watched the Police arrive from his vantage point across the road from the Country Club. He felt safe with a sense of achievement. He pulled the phone from his pocket and pressed Athol D'Large's number.

"Hey, how are things back east?" Athol was always his positive self.

"I've got the particulars you wanted," Kevin said staring at the paper in his hand.

"Ok I'm in the office I'll go to the Department of Motor Registry computer site and put them in." There was a pause. "Things still going swimmingly?" The sarcastic cliché filled in the gap while the computer found the site. "Right let's go."

Kevin Tucker read the four groups of numbers and waited.

"It's a burgundy WH Statesman currently registered in N.S.W. to a Sandy Horder, previously registered to a Emit Horsley in Western Australia and bingo before that John Thomas Johnson. Got 'em." Athol yells down the phone in excitement.

"Ok, you've done well I'm coming over, tomorrow. I'll pick up a car in Sydney and be up there in the afternoon."

"I can do better than that. There's a regional Airport at Williamtown, half an hour away." Kevin advised.

"I'll check out the flights."

Athol's words went into the air when Kevin was interrupted by the old gentleman from earlier with the linen coat and trimmed moustache.

"The salvage is back."

"What!" Kevin twisted his face and looked at the old man.

"The salvage boat, she's coming through the heads," the old gentleman shook his arm and pointed.

Kevin took the phone from his ear and squinted across the bay.

"Those expeditions can last up to two weeks." The gentleman muttered as walked off.

"Are you still there?" Athol called out wondering what the hell was going on.

"Ah, yeah."

"What was that about?"

"Ah, I don't know."

"I'll ring you about the flight." Athol hung up.

Kevin Tucker watched the old man cross the road in front of the Country Club. When he turned back Derrick Fullerton and Bruno walked along the path in front of him looking at the heads. "What are they doing back here?"

★★★★★★★★★★

THE SKIES HAD CLEARED over the *Sugar Bay* , there were two men in the water. After much deliberation it was decided Steve would go back down only if Sandy went with him. The boat had been moved off the site; the explosion had been activated and then placed directly over the wreck, which the view finder now showed as two distinct sections.

Everyone had their job. Maurice was on the communication rope and was the timer as both men only had about half a tank of air each. The other men were at the ready with the chains. In six minutes the chain stopped, there was a pull on the rope.

"They've made it," Maurice exclaimed, "that's half the air."

The boys on the deck looked at each other, doubtingly.

The cage door dropped, the scene had changed. Through the mist of sea sand, the once proud cruiser lay broken badly in two. There was a frenzy of sea life, schools of dead fish floated to the surface. Steve was horrified at the destruction he had caused. There was no time to ponder. He grabbed the lifting chain, tapped Sandy on the shoulder and headed to the wreck.

The two divers approached the wreck from the stern. As they got closer Steve could see the huge damage made was favourable to them. The forward part of the stern had been peeled back, leaving the chest sitting on the sea floor. He led Sandy straight to it, and with a series of hand signals asked Sandy to stand guard while he fixed the chain with a 'D' bolt.

Two sharks flicked in from the side of the broken up forward section. Sandy stood his ground. With no time to alert Steve he held the gun straight and took out the leading predator. Two more came over the top of the wreck before Steve realized. He held the now fixed chain and beckoned Sandy back to the cage.

The dangers of the deep mulled around their own allowing the two men time to reach the sanctuary of the cage. Steve Flint pushed Sandy in first, then tied the chain to the side of the module and pulled the rope twice; he scrambled to get in as the boys up top started the lifting.

The grey fearsome image materialized out of the still unsettled murky depths, it bumped the rear of the cage tumbling both occupants into the open water. Sandy caught hold of the slowly swinging door and watched his friend grope wildly at the water trying to get to the cover of the wreck.

The men on the deck couldn't know what was going on below and pulled the cage chain with all their might. The upward thrust jerked Sandy's head away from seeing the carnage that went on below him.

When the cage broke the surface Sandy was still clinging to the open door. Muscat, who was crouched on the rear landing reached out to help his friend. Before anybody thought there was trouble, the crazed shark flew out of the depths took the Italian and crashed through the side railing of the *Sugar Bay* in a mad horrifying act.

CHAPTER 31

AFTER THE TRAGEDY

"There are three elderly men in deep shock, one of them is insulin dependent, and he's pretty serious." Sandy explained over the radio.

"We'll be out there in forty minutes Captain, have I got the coordinates right?"

Marine rescue read the two sets of numbers. Sandy knew them by heart.

"That's right."

"Do you have medication for the patient on insulin?"

"Yes."

"Keep a close eye on him. Is there anyone you want us to contact?" the sensitive operator asked.

"We've lost two men, this is hard," Sandy's voice broke as he wore all the blame.

"It will be in the hands of the Water Police. They'll send a boat out to bring you in."

"That won't be necessary, I'll bring the boat in," Sandy said thinking of the consequences.

"No Sir, its protocol, the boat is now a crime scene."

"I see."

"How are they Jimmy?"

"Dominic's a bloody mess, so am I," he sucked in air and looked at Sandy "What just happened?"

"Come on," he led Jimmy down the forward section and stood in the doorway. Maurice Campbell lay on the lounge cum bunk, while Walt McEnroe wiped his brow.

"How's he going?" Sandy gulped. Walt looked to the doorway and said nothing. "The helicopter is on its way."

Back up on the bridge and alone Sandy Horder looked at a grim future. As Captain, he was now responsible for the loss of two lives at sea. The investigation will dig up his past. It won't be the embarrassment; it will be the huge amount of money that can't be accounted for. It will be imprisonment.

Two helicopters lifted four men off the *Sugar Bay* at sea, and left Sandy and Jimmy alone and waiting. "What do we do?" Jimmy asked.

Sandy hadn't said anything about the conversation he had with sea rescue. Nobody knew the real story and nobody ever would. "We have to take care of things; first we have to bring up the cage and the chest. We've got to secure it."

They got the cage on board easily enough but struggled with the heavy awkward chest.

Sandy undid the cradle from around the chest then got his tool box and prized open an old lock.

"What are you doing?" Jimmy was in shock he wanted no more excitement. He needed to grieve.

"Get the orb and the knife Steve brought up on the first dive," Sandy ordered.

Jimmy went to the forward section and got the two items from the storage under the seat next to the galley. On the floor of the storage cupboard laid the sixteen small neatly tied bags of diamonds. The youngest crew member looked around the small confine that was once a place of jubilance and expectations. It was now a place of wealth and gloom.

Jimmy stepped out of the hatch onto the deck to see Sandy sitting next to the open chest. It was crammed with the past that few people could imagine. A history of only elite minds could value and the wrath of which took two good men's lives.

Without saying anything Sandy took the items from the younger man and placed them on top of the spoils. He closed the lid and slipped a quarter inch bolt and nut through the clasp.

"Let's get this into the cage."

"Why are we doing this?" it was all over for Jimmy. He didn't want any of this anymore. He wanted his old life back. He needed to grieve for his old life. He wanted to grieve for the life of the friends he just lost. Life could never be the same after today.

Sandy could see what was going on. He encouraged Jimmy to rest.

Once he was on his own he dragged the chest into the cage and did up the 'D' bolt, then went up onto the bridge and started the engines. Against all conventions he left the area and took a wide arc on the way back to port. He didn't want to see anyone until his work was done.

Sandy Horder on the bridge of his prized cruiser with the wind in his face knew now how the Captain of the other fateful cruiser felt, with the treasure on board and nowhere to hide, and people about to bear down.

The radio came on it was the Water Police, they wanted his position. The sound of the radio which contrasted with the drone of the two marine engines stirred Jimmy who had wandered onto the deck. "We're still at the spot." He replied giving false information. "Where are you people now?"

"We're just out of the heads," the Water Police gave the lateral line which would coincide with the spot where the Sugar Bay should have been, "we'll be there in forty five minutes." Sandy turned the screen on and adjusted his route out two more squares. He pulled the lever back to compensate for the extra distance he would have to travel.

From the main deck Jimmy heard the conversation and felt the extra thrust when Sandy leaned on the power. He looked over at the chest now locked in the cage.

CHAPTER 32

BRINGING IT HOME

Kevin Tucker turned to look back at the Country Club and watched the old man in the linen coat with the trimmed moustache walk into the cane lounge of the reputable establishment.

'What did he have to lose?' he thought, the old bloke likes a chat. With that Kevin walked across the road to chew the fat with his new best friend.

"Oh hello again," Kevin opened up proceedings when he headed to the old man's table. "Ah, do you mind if I sit?" he indicated the vacant chair.

"Yes, of course, of course."

"Oh good, good," Kevin echoed, smiled and hoped the old bloke didn't think he was mimicking him. "I'm up from Sydney to meet an old friend," Kevin hesitated, "he's staying here I believe."

"What's his name, what's his name?"

"Sandy." Kevin feigned a cough.

"Sandy Horder? Sandy Horder?" the old man's face lit up.

"Oh you know him?" that's all the information the sleuth's helper needed.

"Everyone knows Sandy, everyone knows Sandy, funny, I haven't seen him for some time. Probably a week or more, or more." With that the old man leaned back in his chair and

interrupted a perfectly sane conversation going on behind.
"Jack, Jack, have you seen Sandy around the last couple of
days, days."

"No, no."

Shit there's an echo in here and it's catching, the sleuth's
offsider smiled and put his hand to his forehead.

"The boat's been gone over a week." Jack finished off.

"So it has, so it has." The old man turned back to Kevin. He
looked and pointed through the glass.

"If you line that round pillar up out the front," the old
gentleman pointed again, "with the heads there's a mooring
point three parts of the way out. The *Sugar Bay* is usually
moored there."

Now I know there's a boat, Kevin Tucker ticked that one
off.

"Yes he told me he had bought a boat."

"Oh he's had for a long time, long time, beautiful boat
beautiful boat. Isn't it Jack?"

"What?"

"Sandy's boat, it's a beautiful boat, beautiful boat, isn't it?"

"Oh yeah, yeah."

"Yes, he goes out with Maurice Campbell and the boys
fishing, every Thursday, every Thursday."

"Today's Friday."

"That's right, that's right. Don't know what's going on,
what's going on."

****

"THAT'S WHAT WE'VE got to do son," Sandy said to
Jimmy on the bridge of the *Sugar Bay* as he negotiated the

tricky waters of the heads, "it's hard at this time I know, but we've got to hide it, let someone find it another day."

"Don't you think we should hand it over?"

"To who?" Sandy looked at a good friend, someone who had been through hell with him.

"The authorities."

"What authorities? Some Government Department will confiscate what we brought back and tie it up in bureaucratic nonsense for years. I'd rather drop it in the ocean now."

Jimmy wanted no more of the coveted trophy. This chest in the cage at the back of the boat that cost two friends lives.

"Ok so we push it off at the mooring. What do we tell the Police though Sandy?"

"The Police won't know about the treasure, I doubt the other boys will mention it. We've kept the secret thus far."

"And the others?" Jimmy asked.

"I've got a story ending for them."

The *Sugar Bay* idled around the front of the mooring point. Sandy lifted the edge of the cage and rolled it into the bay. He watched the bubbles rise then, looked to the panorama of Shoal Bay knowing that this was his last day in paradise.

Without a word he strode up to the bridge engaged the drive and cruised to the waiting throng at the wharf.

★★★★★★★★★★

LIKE A LOT OF THE townsfolk Kevin Tucker walked out on the wharf to see what all the to do was about when the *Sugar Bay* docked.

The 'Sugar Bay' the boat he had learned earlier was the name of the boat owned by Sandy Horder.

He saw a distinguished man well dressed in an aqua polo shirt and white chinos, who wore comfortable tan moccasins and shaded his face with a Country Club emblazoned cap.

"Who is that man?" Kevin asked as he moved to the front of the crowd.

"That's Sandy Horder."

"That's Sandy Horder?" Kevin looked at the scruffy fisherman beside him. "What's going on?"

"Something happened out there," the fisherman nodded towards the heads. "that's why the Water Police are here."

"What happened?" Kevin's investigation was gathering momentum.

"Dunno. The cops are boarding his boat."

"Mr. Horder you were to stay at the site. We have a Police boat on its way out there now with Sargent Bryant on board."

"Don't expect us to stay out there. I'm here to see the crew and their families. What's the latest on Maurice Campbell?"

"We'll have to impound the boat." The Water Police officer said.

"Do what you have to do." Sandy patted Jimmy on the shoulder. "Come on son."

They pushed through the growing crowd to the street.

"I've got to go Jimmy." Without any explanation the two split up.

Neither Jimmy nor any of his old fishing mates ever saw Sandy Horder again.

****

A LONE FIGURE walked toward the end of the wharf at Shoal Bay at three o'clock the next morning. It is the hour of bandits and cheats. Neither title suited this man. He lifted the yellow Police tape around the Sugar Bay stepped aboard and found the key under the cushion of the Captain's seat on the bridge.

The twin Volvo marine engines rumbled quietly when they weren't encouraged with the throttle. It was set just enough so that it would slowly but surely move silently through the water out into the middle of the bay.

A burgundy Statesman stopped at the Salamander round-about at four thirty, before dawn. A smart looking man got out and looked back towards Port Stephens. He looked at his watch. He waited.

In fifteen minutes there was a bright glow in the sky. He got back in his car and drove off.

CPSIA information can be obtained
at www.ICGtesting.com
Printed in the USA
BVHW030210240921
617454BV00006B/55

9 781649 699602